Frank Collins Baker

A Naturalist in Mexico

being a visit to Cuba, northern Yucatan and Mexico

Frank Collins Baker

A Naturalist in Mexico
being a visit to Cuba, northern Yucatan and Mexico

ISBN/EAN: 9783337378721

Printed in Europe, USA, Canada, Australia, Japan

Cover: Foto ©Andreas Hilbeck / pixelio.de

More available books at **www.hansebooks.com**

— -A -

NATURALIST IN MEXICO

BEING A VISIT TO

CUBA, NORTHERN YUCATAN
AND MEXICO.

WITH MAPS AND ILLUSTRATIONS.

BY

FRANK COLLINS BAKER,

SECRETARY AND CURATOR, CHICAGO ACADEMY OF SCIENCES;
FELLOW OF THE ROCHESTER ACADEMY OF SCIENCES;
MEMBER OF THE AMERICAN ASSOCIATION OF CONCHOLOGISTS; OF THE
CHICAGO ACADEMY OF SCIENCES;
ASSOCIATE MEMBER OF THE AMERICAN ORNITHOLOGISTS UNION.

AUTHOR OF

" A Catalogue of the Echinodermata;" "Catalogue and Synonomy of the
Muricidæ;" "Catalogue of Mexican Mollusks," Etc., Etc.

CHICAGO:
DAVID OLIPHANT, PRINTER AND PUBLISHER.
1895

PREFACE.

In presenting this little volume to the public, a word or two in explanation of the circumstances which gave it birth may not be deemed inappropriate. The author had originally intended making a little pamphlet covering some of the more interesting experiences of the Mexican Expedition. It has been thought, however, that the important nature of the expedition and the linking together of narrative, science, and history (a combination not often attempted by authors) were circumstances sufficient to justify its publication in a more pretentious form.

The tour which forms its subject was undertaken under the auspices of the Academy of Natural Sciences of Philadelphia, the author acting as Zoologist. The expedition was under the leadership of Professor Angelo Heilprin, Curator-in-charge of the Philadelphia Academy, and its object was to collect data and specimens illustrating the fauna, flora, and Geology of Yucatan and Southern Mexico, with a consideration of the high mountain peaks of the Mexican Plateau. For full accounts concerning the scientific portion of the expedition, the reader is respectfully referred to the Proceedings of the above Academy from 1890 to 1895.

The illustrations used are mostly from photographs taken by the party, together with sketches made by the author. The majority of new species of mollusks discovered by the expedition are figured in the following pages.

As to the literary character of the work, if not so good as might be wished, it is yet such as circumstances have permitted. The text has been written during the leisure hours of a busy professional life, which fact will explain, if it does not excuse, its errors. The author has endeavored to picture the scenes which came under his observation, as they appeared to him.

The author desires to express his gratitude to the friends, both in Mexico and the United States, who have in various ways assisted him. He trusts that this little sketch of a naturalists experiences may awaken a scientific interest in this little understood country.

FRANK COLLINS BAKER.

Chicago Academy of Sciences,
July, 1895.

CONTENTS.

CHAPTER VII.

CHAPTER VIII.

CHAPTER IX.

CHAPTER X.

CHAPTER XI.

CHAPTER XII.

CHAPTER XIII.

CHAPTER XIV.

ILLUSTRATIONS.

A NATURALIST IN MEXICO.

CHAPTER I.

We left Philadelphia on the morning of February 15th, and reached New York City to find it clothed in a wintry garb. That afternoon we took passage on board the steamship Orizaba, of the Ward Steamship Company's Line. The mail steamer sailed promptly at the time assigned, hauled out into the stream by a couple of noisy little tugs, with two-inch hawsers made fast to stem and stern. Before sunset the pilot left the ship, which was then headed due south for Cuba. The sharp north-west wind, though blustering and aggressive, was in our favor, and helped us not a little on our journey. We doubled Cape Hatteras and Cape Lookout well in towards the shore, sighting on the afternoon of the third day the Island of Abaco, largest of the Bahama Isles. The woolen clothing worn when we came on board ship had already become oppressive, the cabin thermometer indicating 75° Fahrenheit. With nothing to engage the eye save the blue sky and the bluer water, the most is made of every circumstance at sea, and even trivial occurrences become notable. The playful dolphins went through their aquatic pantomines for our amusement. Half a dozen of them started off just ahead of the cut-water, and raced the ship for two hours, keeping exactly the same relative distance ahead without any apparent effort. The broken main-mast of a ship, floating, with considerable top hamper attached, was passed, suggestive of a recent wreck.

The voyager in these latitudes is constantly saluted by gentle breezes impregnated with tropical fragrance, intensified in effect by the distant view of palmetto trees, clothing the islands and growing down to the water's very edge. As we glide along, little groups of flying-fish are seen enjoying an air bath, either in frolic or in fear; pursued, may be, by some aquatic enemy, to escape from whom they essay these aerial flights. On the port side may be seen the dim outline of the Bahamas. Here is the harvest field of the conchologist, the beaches and coral reefs affording an abundant supply of exquisitely colored shells of many different species.

It was interesting to remain on deck at night and watch the heavens, as we glided silently through the phosphorescent sea. Was it possible the grand luminary, which rendered objects so plain that one could almost read fine print with no other help, shone solely by borrowed light? We all know it to be so, and also that Venus, Mars, Jupiter, and Saturn shine in a similar manner with light reflected from the sun.

We were now running through the Florida Straits, where one branch of the Gulf Stream finds its way northward. The Gulf Stream! Who can explain the mystery of its motive power; what keeps its tepid waters in a course of thousands of miles from mingling with the rest of the sea; whence does it come? The accepted theories are familiar enough, but it is hard to believe them.

On the morning of the fourth day we sighted the Island of Cuba, and studied its long, bold outline. Soon after sighting the island, the famous Moro Castle is seen. This antique, yellow, Moorish-looking stronghold is picturesque to the last degree, with its crumbling, honeycombed battlements, and queer little flanking turrets, grated windows, and shadowy towers. It is built upon the face of a lofty,

dun-colored rock, upon whose precipitous side the fortifica-
tion is terraced. It stands just at the entrance of the narrow channel leading to the city, so that in passing in, one
can easily exchange greetings with the sentry on the outer
battlement.

On the opposite shore the battery of La Punta stands
guard over that side of the channel. Passing through the
narrow channel between these two fortifications we entered
the harbor, steamed up the strait to where it widens into a
basin, made fast to a buoy, and had our first glimpse of
cocoa-palms. Some harbor-boats took us ashore. We
landed at broad stone steps pervaded by smells, passed into
the Custom House, and out of it into paved lanes full of
donkeys, negroes, soldiers, sellers of fruit and lottery-tick-
ets, engaged in transactions in a debased fractional currency.
The money of the debt-ridden island is that of our "shin-
plaster" war period. A couple of boiled eggs in a common
restaurant cost forty cents; a ride in a horse-car thirty-five.
The wages of a minor clerk at the same time were but $40
or $50 a month. How does he make ends meet and pro-
vide for his future?

Havana is a thoroughly representative city—Cuban and
nothing else. Its history embraces in no small degree that
of all the island, being the center of its talent, wealth, and
population. The harbor, or bay, is shaped like one's out-
spread hand, with the wrist for an entrance, and is populous
with the ships of all nations. It presents at all times a
scene of great maritime activity. Besides the national ships
of other countries and those of Spain, mail steamers from
Europe and America are coming and going daily; also
coasting steamers from the eastern and southern shores of
the island, added to regular lines for Mexico and the islands of the Caribbean Sea. The large ferry steamers plying constantly between the city and the Regla shore, the

fleet of little sailing boats, foreign yachts, and row-boats, glancing in the burning sunlight, created a scene of great maritime interest.

The city presents a large extent of public buildings, cathedrals, antique and venerable churches. There is nothing grand in its appearance as one enters the harbor and comes to anchor. Its multitude of churches, domes, and steeples are not architecturally remarkable, and are dominated by the colossal prison near the shore. This immense quadrangular edifice flanks the Punta, and is designed to contain five thousand prisoners at a time. The low hills which make up the distant background are not sufficiently high to add much to the general effect. The few palm trees which catch the eye here and there give an Oriental aspect to the scene, quite in harmony with the atmospheric tone of intense sunshine. Neither the city nor its immediate environs is elevated, so that the whole impression is that of flatness, requiring some strength of background to form a complete picture.

The low-lying, many-colored city of Havana was originally surrounded by a wall, though the population has long since extended its dwellings and business structures far into what was, half a century since, the suburbs. A portion of the old wall is still extant, crumbling and decayed, but it has mostly disappeared. The narrow streets are paved or macadamized, and cross each other at right angles, like those of Philadelphia. There are no sidewalks, unless a narrow line of flagstones can be so called, and in fact the people have less use for them where nearly every one rides in a victoria, the fare being but sixteen cents per mile.

The architecture of the dwelling-houses is exceedingly heavy, giving them the appearance of great age. They are built of the porous stone so abundant upon the island, which, though soft when at first worked into suitable blocks, becomes as hard as granite by exposure to the atmosphere. The façades of the town houses are nearly always covered with stucco. The dwelling houses are universally so constructed as to form an open square in the center, which constitutes the only yard, or court, that is attached. The house is divided into a living room, a store-room, chambers, and stable, all upon one floor. If there is a second story, a broad flight of steps leads to it, and there are the family chambers, or sleeping apartments, opening upon a corridor which extends round the court.

The Botanical Garden, one of the many attractions of Havana, is situated about a mile from the city proper, adjoining which are the attractive grounds of the Governor-General's country house. Both are open to the public and richly repay a visit. The Governor's grounds are shaded by a great variety of tropical trees and flowers. Altogether, the place is a wilderness of blossoms composed of exotic and native flowers. There is also an interesting aviary to be seen here, and a small artificial lake is covered with web-footed birds and brilliant-feathered ducks. The gardens seem to be neglected, but they are very lovely in their native luxuriance. Dead wood and decaying leaves are always a concomitant of such gardens in the low latitudes. Here is a great variety of the scarlet hibiscus and the garland of night, which grows like a young palm to eight or nine feet, throwing out from the center of its drooping foliage a cluster of brown blossoms tipped with white, shaped like a mammoth bunch of grapes. It blooms at night, and is fragrant only by moon and starlight.

Late in the afternoon of the 21st we left Havana, and turned our prow toward Progreso, Yucatan, expecting to arrive there on the 23rd. The nights of the latter part of February in this latitude were exceedingly beautiful, and solemnly impressive was the liberal splendor of the sky. The full moon looked down upon and was reflected by waters of perfect smoothness. The air was as mild as June in Pennsylvania, while at night the Southern Cross and the North Star blazed in the horizon at the same time. As we steered westward, after leaving Havana, both of these heavenly sentinels were seen abeam, the constellation on our port side and the North Star on our starboard.

On the morning of the 23rd we reached Progreso, and came to anchor four miles from shore. It was necessary to keep at this distance on account of the extreme shallowness of the water, and, also, to be in readiness for the sudden advent af a norther. We procured a shore boat to take us and our baggage on shore, and landed at a wharf covered with bales of hemp and brown-skinned natives with white suits on. The customs examinations were soon passed, and we were at liberty to go wherever our own will should lead us.

Progreso, like some of our new western cities, is better laid out than settled. It has its straight, broad streets running through chaparral, its grand plaza, with scarcely a corner of it yet occupied, and its corner lots at fabulous prices. The market-place is a projecting, thatched roof over the side of a one-story edifice. On mats sit brown old ladies, with almost equally old-looking vegetables. Here are oranges, bananas, black beans, squash seeds boiled in molasses, a sort of candy, and other esculents, to us unknown.

The houses of Progreso are of one story, of mortar or thatch, covered with a high roof of thatch. This high roof is open inside, and makes them shady and cool. The sides are also often of thatch, and they look like a brown dwarf with a huge, brown straw sombrero pulled over his eyes. Some of these built of mortar have ornamental squares in the sides, where shells are carefully set in various shapes in the mortar, and which make a pleasing effect, the diamonds and other shapes giving the walls a variety that is really artistic. Here I first tasted the sort of chocolate of which Montezuma was so fond. A brown, brawny Indian made us a cup of the same in a corner café. It is prepared in milk, and is a thick, soft liquid that melts on your tongue. One must come to Mexico to know how "chocolatte" can taste.

The fields about Progreso have chiefly shrubs and cacti. Beautiful flowers of purple, yellow, and crimson abound. Here the heliotrope grows wild, the fragrant purple flower that is scattered so generally at funerals. The sweet-pea and other cultivated delights of the northern hot-house and garden, are blooming abundantly.

The cocoa-palm throws out its long spines, deep green, thrust straight out from a gray trunk, that looks as if wrapped in old clothes against the cold. This gray bark is a striking offset to the dark, rich leaves, which are the branches themselves. Where these leaves push forth from the trunk, from ten to fifty feet from the ground, a cluster of green balls, of various sizes and ages, is hanging. Then the black shell known to us is reached, and inside of that, not the thick, white substance we find on opening it, but a thin, soft layer, or third rind, the most of the hollow being filled with milk. Later in the season the milk coagulates to meat, and the cocoanut of commerce is completed.

The people are chiefly natives; not of the Aztec, but Toltec variety. This is a nation hundreds of years older than the Aztecs, and who are supposed to be the builders of the famous monuments of Central America, and to have been driven from Mexico southward about a thousand years ago. Both sexes wear white, the men and boys having often one leg of their trousers rolled up, for what pur-

pose we could not guess, unless it be for the more cleanly
fording of the brooklets and mudlets that occur. The
women wear a skirt of white, and a loose white waist sep-
arate from the skirt, and hanging sometimes near to the
bottom of the under garment. This over-skirt, or robe, is
ornamented with fringe and borders worked in blue. The
head-dress is a shawl, or mantle, of light cotton gauze, of
blue or purple, thrown gracefully over the head and
shoulders.

Before leaving Progreso for Merida we engaged the
services of a Spaniard, Señor Lopez by name, who spoke
English, Spanish, and Maya (the native tongue), to act
as our interpreter during our stay in Yucatan. He proved a
most valuable adjunct to our party. A little before 5 o'clock
P. M. we boarded the train for Merida. Before leaving the
dĕpot we were accosted by a gentleman, who introduced
himself as Colonel Glenn, and who extended to us an invitation to visit his railroad construction camp, situated near
the town of Tekanto. We accepted his kind invitation, and
promised soon to see him and his camp. At 5 o'clock sharp
the train pulled out from Progreso, and we were soon steam-
ing rapidly toward the capital of Yucatan.

The character of the country for some little distance
outside of Progreso was decidedly swampy. A short distance beyond the town we crossed a broad lagoon, in which
was said to abound many species of wild fowl. As our
train sped along, numbers of birds rose upon either side,
and with discordant cries flew deeper into the swamp. I
noticed particularly several large herons, which I judged
were the common Great Blue Heron of our southern
states. Several egrets, and numerous members of the
raptoral, or hawk, order of birds were seen. The land soon
changed from swampy to very dry, and continued thus the
remainder of the journey. In many places whole acres

were seen under cultivation, henequen being the principal article. This henequen, the substance from which the famous Sisal hemp is made, is a Maguey plant (the *Agave Sisalensis* of botanists), and much resembles the plant found on the plains of Apam, in Mexico, from which the celebrated Mexican drink, *pulque*, is made. The growing of henequen is one of the chief industries of Yucatan, if not the chief one. In the distance several ruined mounds were seen, but nothing which gave us the faintest conception of the grand and wonderful buried cities of the interior.

After a two hours' ride we reached Merida, a little after dark. We put up at the Hotel Yucateco, the best hotel in the city, kept by Señor Escalente, a very worthy and obliging gentleman. After supper, eaten in a café kept in a grocery store, we examined more closely our quarters. The rooms were all situated on the ground floor, and were about twenty-five feet in height, twenty in length, and fifteen in width, with a cloth partition extending half-way to the ceiling, making two rooms of one. The furniture consisted of a bed, chair, and wash-stand; the bed clothing of but a pair of sheets!

We were awakened early next morning by the clanging of the bells of the cathedral close by. One of these bells was cracked, and produced a most doleful sound. After making a careful toilet, for it was Sunday, we made a more accurate survey of our surroundings than we were able to do the evening before. Our room looked very prison-like with its barred windows, the early morning light streaming through, and its high, plastered walls. It brought forcibly to mind the pictures I had seen of Columbus in prison. Stepping from our room we entered a spacious court-yard, upon which all the rooms opened. In the center of this court yard was an ancient well, and beside it a modern steam-pump, a strange object to see beside so antique a well.   Several tree-like vines were growing in the court, and upon the ground several bright plumaged birds were feeding.   After eating a light breakfast we left the hotel to look about the city.

Merida is a city of about forty thousand inhabitants, situated twenty miles from Progreso.   It stands on a great plain, on a surface of limestone rock, and the temperature and climate are said to be very uniform.   The general aspect of the city is Moorish, as it was built at a time when the Moorish style prevailed in Spanish architecture.   The houses are large, generally of stone, and one story in height, with balconies to the windows, and large court-yards.   The windows are invariably barred, which give the houses a prison-like aspect.   In the center of the city stands the *plaza major*, or great square.   This is about six hundred feet square.   The east side is occupied by the cathedral and the various quarters of the bishop.   On the north stands a long, low, two-storied building, the lower story occupied by stores, restaurants, and offices.   The upper story is devoted to private dwelling apartments.   On the west is the government municipal building, its front supported upon arches, the long colonnades giving it an imposing appearance, it being a handsome stone building of good dimensions.   On the south is a building which attracted our attention as soon as we entered the plaza.   It is distinguished by a richly-sculptured façade of very curious design.   The subject represents two knights in armor, standing on the shoulders of naked figures, probably representing the conquering Spaniard trampling upon the fallen native.   It is probably native work from Spanish design.   In this façade is a stone with the following inscription:

ESTA OBRA MANDO HACERLA EL

ADELANTADO DON FRANCISCO DE MONTEJO.

AÑO DE MDXLIX.,

which, translated into English, means: "The Adelantado Don Francisco Montejo caused this to be erected in the year 1549." This is said to be one of the oldest buildings in Merida, and also one of the oldest in Yucatan. It was erected five years after the foundation of the city.

Eight streets lead from the plaza, two in the direction of each cardinal point. In every street, at the distance of a few yards, is a gate, now in a state of ruin, and beyond are the suburbs. In the center of the plaza is an object which seems out of place among the old buildings, viz., an electric light, placed at the top of a very high, ladder-like platform. Beneath this electric light "pole" is a beautiful fountain. Seats are placed in convenient places for the comfort of those visiting the plaza. The whole is surrounded by an iron fence.

GATE IN MERIDA.

This plaza was the scene of a great battle, in 1540, between the Spaniards and natives, the latter numbering 70,000, while the former numbered but 200; so says the historian. The natives, however, were defeated, but not until they had killed or wounded nearly all the Spaniards. A large mound once stood on the ground now occupied by the plaza; it was razed to the ground by the Spaniards, and from it, and numerous ancient buildings, the present city of Merida was built.

The great distinguishing feature of Merida, as of all the cities of the Spanish-American countries, is in its churches. The great cathedral, the Church of the Jesuits, the

Church of San Cristoval, the Chapel of San Juan Bautista, and the convent of Mejorada, are all interesting. Many of them are of good style of architecture, and rich in ornaments. Of the many churches of the city, the cathedral, situated, as before said, on the east side of the plaza, is the largest and most interesting. While the service was yet in progress we entered and stood near the door, the better to study the interior. At the extreme end stood the altar, upon a raised platform about thirty feet in height, elaborately carved and ornamented. Upon either side, in large cases, were life-size wax figures of biblical characters. The organ was situated on the right-hand side. The center of the church rose in a spacious dome of great height. Several priests were officiating at the altar, and the floor of the church was covered with kneeling women dressed in white. Through the entire body of the church not a man was to be seen. The music slowly died away, and the women rose from their knees, appearing like a white cloud; but, as they turned toward the door, the horizon became dusky with black faces, the whole front rank being composed of natives. The Spanish ladies occupied the part of the church immediately in front of the altar. It was a beautiful sight to see that party of pretty native girls, many of whom were of a decidedly handsome cast, slowly file out.

After dinner we walked out one of the streets leading north from the plaza. On either side of the street were the huts of the natives They were built of stone and mortar, and roofed over, or thatched, with palm leaves. Sometimes there was a window, but more often two doors facing each other on opposite sides, and in the center, of the hut. They were set back a few feet from the road, and were, in most cases, surrounded by a stone wall. Inside they contained but one room, with a fire place in one end, and several hammocks swung in the other. At one of these huts we

A GROUP OF NATIVE YUCATECANS.

PLATE II.

secured a photograph of a group of native men, women, and children.

Along the walls, and in the fields bordering the road, we searched for fossils, and succeeded in finding several fine specimens. We found here several fossil mollusks identical with those found in the Caloosahatchie beds of southern Florida. This fact seemed to point toward a later geological period than is generally assigned to Yucatan, and showed it to be clearly related to the Post Pliocene of Florida. We also found large numbers of land shells about the stone walls bordering the road, and occasionally a lively little lizard would start from a crevice and scamper under a projecting rock.

As we penetrated farther into the country, birds, and animal life in general, became more abundant. Bright plumaged birds flew from tree to tree, and gaudy butterflies flitted slowly by. Among the birds we could distinguish such species as the Great tailed Grackle, numerous flycatchers and jays. The most noticeable objects were a number of turkey vultures, who were regaling themselves on the half-eaten carcass of a horse. These vultures are great scavengers, and quickly devour any refuse matter, or dead animal, that is left where they can get at it. They are the chief garbage gatherers of Mexico, and a fine is imposed for killing them. We returned to the city toward nightfall, and spent the evening listening to a very good band in the *plaza major.*

It was in the year 1506 that Juan Dias de Solis discovered the east coast of Yucatan, and sailed along it some distance. On the 8th of February, 1517, Francisco Hernandez de Cordova landed at Cape Cotoche, was attacked by the natives, and a battle ensued, in which the latter were repulsed with great slaughter. They next landed at Campeachy, and noted a city there composed of stone houses.   They next landed at a town called Champoton for water, and a terrific battle took place between the Spaniards and natives, in which fifty seven Spaniards were killed and many wounded.   On the 6th of April, 1518, another expedition, under command of Juan de Grijalva, set forth, and discovered the Island of Cozumel.   They landed at Champoton, called by the Spaniards Bay *de Mal a Pelea*, or "of the bad fight," and another battle ensued, in which the Spaniards were compelled to retreat to their ships.

In the year 1527, Don Francisco Montejo set sail from Seville in four vessels, with four hundred men, for the conquest of Yucatan.   They landed at the Island of Cozumel, took a native for an interpreter, sailed to the mainland, and landed all the Spanish soldiers.   Under the guidance of the native from Cozumel they marched along the coast, and, without receiving any resistance from the natives, arrived at Conil.   From Conil the expedition marched to the province of Choaca, and from there to Aké, where they were con-fronted by a multitude of natives.   Here a fearful battle ensued, which lasted two days, and ended in the defeat of the natives with more than 1,200 of their number killed.   From Aké the Spaniards went to Chichen Itza.   Here the Adelantado divided his forces, and sent Captain Davila with sixty-six men to Ba Khalal.   Those left at Chichen Itza were soon in a very desperate condition.   An immense multitude of natives having assembled before them, the Spaniards sallied forth, and a terrific battle followed.   Great slaughter was made among the natives, and one hundred and fifty Spaniards were killed.

Two years later, Captain Davila and the Adelantado, after much suffering, met again at Campeachy.   The sufferings of the little band at Campeachy were terrible, and after enduring the hardships until all but five were reduced to sickness, they abandoned the place.

We next hear of the attempt to conquer the country by converting the natives to Christianity. The Franciscan Friar, Jacob de Festera, with four companions, set out to convert the country. This project, after a trial, failed.

In 1537, the Adelantado again landed in Yucatan, at Champoton, where another terrific battle took place. For several years the Spaniards remained at this place. In 1539, the Adelantado put in the hands of his son the pacification of Yucatan. Again setting out, the Spaniards marched from Champoton to Campeachy, their line of march being marked by numerous battles with the natives. Don Francisco now sent his cousin, Captain Francisco de Montejo, into Quepech, to found a city in the native town of Tihoo. In the year 1540 he arrived at Tihoo. Here occurred one of the most sanguinary battles of the conquest, 70,000 natives against 200 Spaniards, in which the natives were defeated with great slaughter. The caciques, finding it impossible to drive the Spaniards from the country, came to Don Francisco with offers of peace. On the 6th of January, 1542, on the site of the native town of Tihoo, the very "loyal and noble" city of Merida was founded. Five years later the curious house was built of which we before spoke. From that time to the present the Spanish speaking people have held undisputed sway in Yucatan.

We spent the following day in looking about the city. Under the guidance of a gentleman whom we had met at the hotel, we traversed the city in every direction. Of especial interest to us were the *cenotes,* or natural wells. One which we visited was situated in the rear of a grocery in the northern part of the city. It was thirty-five feet in depth from the surface of the earth to that of the water, and the latter, in its deepest part, measured about five feet. Leading from the surface to the floor of the *cenote* was a stone stair-case, well worn as though it had been much used in times past. On the sides of the well were stone benches, and in one end the floor shelved down to the water's edge. The water was of a bluish color, and had a taste of sulphur. This *cenote*, its roof and base, was an immense fossil formation. Marine shells were conglomerated together in solid masses, many of the shells being very perfect. It was used for bathing purposes during the dry season, and also to furnish water to the inhabitants.

While returning to our hotel we passed several natives with bundles of ramon, or fodder, on their backs. They were known as *venedors de ramon*, or sellers of ramon, and they seemed to do a thriving business. Several *calesas* containing handsome señoras and señoritas were also passed. These *calesas* were drawn by a single horse or mule, the driver being perched on his back, and were very curious and interesting vehicles.

A visit to Merida is not complete without visiting the market. This is situated in the southern part of the town, and is a large and roomy building. Here were displayed for sale all kinds of meats, vegetables, fruits, sweetmeats, toys, wearing apparel, and in fact about everything to be found in Yucatan. The servants of the well-to-do people were here getting their daily provisions. One young native woman I noticed particularly. With her were two small children, and at her breast was a young child apparently about nine months old. She was very pretty, with a shapely head covered with an abundant growth of glossy black hair. Her features were regular, and her form graceful and symmetrical in outline. She wore the usual dress of the native population. This consisted of a skirt, called a *pic*, extending from the waist to the ankles, and an outside over-skirt, or *uipil*, extending from the shoulders to the knees. It was cut low in the neck, was without sleeves, and elaborately embroidered. She was barefooted and bareheaded. `

In the eastern part of the city is situated a second, but much smaller market, where the merchants, if such they may be called, sit cross-legged before a piece of straw matting, upon which is displayed for sale beans, maize, fruits, etc. Here, also, is the abode of the pottery and leather trade in Merida.

Near this smaller market is the old Franciscan convent, built on the site of an ancient temple. It stands on an eminence, and is enclosed by a high stone wall, now in ruins. It is now called the *Castillo*, and is used as barracks for a regiment of soldiery. It was once a powerful factor among the people, and its walls sheltered three hundred Franciscan monks; but by the new constitution obtained by the revolutionists in Spain, in 1820, the monks were driven out, their order destroyed, and they themselves obliged to flee for their lives. Inside the convent the noise of an anvil could be heard, and several Mestizos were seen at a blacksmith's forge. This convent contains one memorial of far more interest than the old convent. In one of the corridors going north is seen that peculiar arch so puzzling to archæologists—two sides rising to meet each other, and covered, when within about a foot of each other, by a flat layer of stones.

On the afternoon of our third day in Merida we left that city for Tekanto to visit Col. Glenn's railway camp, he having reported that region as abounding in interest to the naturalist and antequarian. The scenery was the same as that about Merida—flat and dry. At dusk we reached Tekanto, and were met there by the colonel's locomotive, which was to convey us from the latter place to the construction camp. A twenty minutes' ride brought us to the camp, and we alighted in front of a freight-car, in which a bountiful supper, and the colonel also, was waiting to receive us. While the meal was in progress we took a mental inventory of our surroundings.   It was an ordinary freight-car turned into a house.   In each end were two cot beds, in the center the table at which we were eating, and about the walls hung hats, coats, guns, and other objects.   Three lamps with powerful reflectors gave us ample light.

After supper we paid our respects to Mrs. Glenn, an estimable lady, who was braving the hardships of a con-struction camp that she might be with her husband.   As we walked from our "dining" car to that occupied by the colonel, we passed the camp of the men engaged on the construction.   Fires were burning, and groups of men standing or lying about them.   Here was a group amusing itself singing songs, there another listening to the jokes or stories of one of its members·   The night was beautifully clear, and objects about us could be as plainly distinguished as by day.   The queen of night sailed high in the heavens, which were bespangled with millions of stars.   Having paid our respects to the "lady of the camp," we returned to our car and were soon in the "arms of Morpheus."

CHAPTER II.

We were awakened by the shrill whistle of the locomotive, summoning the men to their labors. All was bustle
and confusion. The men were gathered about the water-
tank, performing their morning toilet. Breakfast was soon
announced, and the men rushed pell mell to their seats at a
long table. They fell to eating with a will, and for some
time nothing was heard but the steady click, click of the
knives against the plates. Soon they had emptied their
plates and eaten everything within reach, and were calling
for more. One tall negro at the foot of the table rose, and
pulling from its sheath a knife, or *machete*, flourished it in
the air, shouting at the same time, "Heah, waiter, bring
some moah meat heah, or I'll scalp yer!" At this there was
a general laugh among the men.

The colonel's men were of a rather mixed character as
regarded nationality. There were English, Scotch, Irish,
Germans, Americans, Spaniards, Negroes and Yucatecans; in
fact, Col. Glenn boasted of having about every nation represented in his camp. They were dressed in all manner of
costumes, from old, half-worn-out black suits to overalls
and jumpers.

After breakfast I took my gun, and made an excursion
into the woods near the camp. The morning was beautiful, the air crisp, and birds plentiful, and I had not been
absent from camp but a short time before I had my pockets
filled with small birds. One of the first objects which
greeted me was a beautiful bird I had not hitherto met
with, namely, the Yucatan Cardinal Grosbeak, flocks of
which I saw sporting about the low bushes. It was a small ·
bird with bright red plumage. It was a glorious morning,

the sun not having risen high enough to be uncomfortable; the air had a balmy smell, and the woods teemed with animal life; everything seemed here to delight the heart of the naturalist. The country about the colonel's camp was flat, dry, and covered with a growth of low bushes; but few large trees were seen. The woods abounded with woodpeckers, jays, crotophagas, and hawks. One fact which I noticed particularly was the scarcity of insect life. Hardly an insect was to to be seen, save an occasional butterfly or spider. About the roots of trees I found heaps of land shells, but all were dead.

During one of our excursions we ran across a flock of Ocellated Turkeys, but did not succeed in obtaining a specimen. This species is quite rare, and specimens are much needed in our museums,

On the afternoon of the 28th we engaged a volan and driver, and started on a journey toward Valladolid. This volan, or *volan coche*, as the Yucatecans called it, was a heavy, clumsy affair, but admirably adapted for the rough roads of the country. It was supported upon two large wooden wheels, about as heavy as those used upon our trucks, placed at either end of an eight-foot axle. Upon this axle was a frame-work like our ice-cart covers, supported by a heavy wooden frame. There were no springs, and the jolting was something awful. It was drawn by three diminutive burros.

The driver, whom we christened, for want of a better name, "Isaac McGinty," was a little, dried-up native of uncertain age. He had the usual coppery color and small stature of the Maya people, and was of a most taciturn disposition, His dress consisted of white jacket and pants, sandals, kept in place by a string drawn between the great toe and the next, and a *scrape*, or blanket, of many colors, drawn tightly about his person. These scrapes seemed to be quite a favorite object of wearing apparel with the Yucatecans, and the brighter and more varied the colors, the better was the garment liked.

The day was most brilliant; the sky without a cloud. In fact, it was one of those glorious days preceding the rainy season. The radiation of heat from the limestone road was visible by the quivering motion of the air about it. We saw and heard but few birds; a few cattle, belonging to a hacienda near by, were seen congregating beneath the friendly shelter of a wide-spreading tree. The very soil was warm beneath our feet, and we were exceedingly re-lieved to reach a large hacienda, about noon, where we halted to rest, eat our lunch, and slake our burning thirst.

This hacienda was devoted principally to the cultiva-tion of henequen. This henequen is first cut from the stem quite near the ground, then carried to the mill where it is torn into shreds by machinery, and then hung upon rails in the sun to dry, after which it is put up in bales which are compressed by machinery. The whole process is at once simple and effective, and a great quantity may be baled in a single day. The henequen arrives at maturity, or at a point ready for cutting, in from five to seven years. The leaves, when at their best, are from four to five feet in length. Each plant yields 20 or 30 leaves yearly for a pe-riod of 12 to 20 years, about a third more in the rainy than in the dry season. It takes over 8,000 leaves to make a 400-pound bale. The bales vary in weight from 350 to 450 pounds each.

We ate our lunch beneath the friendly shade of a *ceiba* tree near an old well, from which the water was drawn by means of an endless chain of buckets, propelled by a long pole acting upon a series of wooden cogs. Here I tasted for the first time the *sepote*, a fruit resembling our peach, of which I had heard much. It was very sweet and quite delicious. While eating our lunch several native women came to the well, bearing *cantaros,* or water-jars, to draw water. They made a scene fit for a painter, dressed in their characteristic costume, standing beside the old well. From this hacienda we could see the large mound at Izamal, which was once used as a place of sacrifice by the ancient inhabitants.

Again starting on our journey we passed through the plaza at Izamal, and entered a road leading to a little town called Sitilpech, in which we wished to pass the night. At the distance of a league we passed a fine hacienda, and at half-past five reached the village of Sitilpech, seven leagues from Tekanto. This village consisted of a few native huts, a couple of stone buildings facing the plaza, and an old Spanish church. The population was mostly native, very few of whom spoke anything but Maya. There was not a white man in the place. The village had but one principal street, which was the road over which we came, and which passed through the square near the church. We rode through the street without meeting a single person. Crossing the plaza we entered a grocery store, and obtained permission to store our baggage for the night; we also secured a good supper of beans, soup, and tortillas. Not being able to secure accommodations in any of the huts, we made our beds on the ground in front of the church, and soon fell asleep.

We awoke with sore and aching limbs, but, withal, ready for a fresh start. Early in the day the clouds gathered and the rain came down in torrents, completely drenching us. Not wishing to lose a day on account of the rain, we hitched up and followed the road eastward. We passed down a long street leading through the suburbs of the village; beyond this our road lay across a tract of country, wild and stony, covered with the same vegetation noticed about Col-

Glenn's camp. Following this road for about two miles we reached a cross-road, into which we turned. Here the vegetation changed to a thick and luxuriant forest of *turpentine, ceiba,* and other large trees. Orchids were to be seen here in abundance, as well as numerous climbing plants. This luxuriance of vegetation indicated the presence of some body of water in the vicinity. Nor were we mistaken; for in a few minutes we reached a point in the road, on each side of which was a large body of water enclosed in a circular basin about one thousand feet in diameter, and some thirty feet below the level of the road. These were known as the twin *cenotes,* and were called *Shkolak* and *Skashek.*

These *cenotes* were surrounded by dense vegetation, in which numerous birds were seen. Several snow-white egrets flew off as we approached, and several other species were seen standing about the margins of the pool. The water was filled with a kind of water-lily. Among the birds which inhabited this spot was the Mexican Jacana. It would start up at our approach and fly over the water, with its long feet stretched out behind, uttering a plaintive cry which was pitiful to hear. This bird was apparently quite common, but none were captured.

Several other birds started up as we worked our way through the vegetation, and one, which I had a good view of, seemed to be the *Ardea carulea,* or Little Blue Heron of the States. In a little cove, under the overhanging bank, I found a species of *Ampullaria* (*A. Yucatanensis*), and a *Planorbis* (*P. Caribæus*). In one portion of the *cenote,* where there were no lily pads, the bottom was covered with small stones, and from these I picked a number of small shells resembling a *Patella* (*Ancylus excentricus*). The banks were strewn with dead land shells, but not a single living land mollusk was to be found. The edge of this *cenote* was bordered by a thick growth of cane, so that shooting was

rather difficult; and, indeed, had we shot any of the birds
we would not have been able to get them, as we had no
boat and did not dare to wade in after them.   Photographs
were taken of both *cenotes*, together with several of the trees
about.

We returned to Sitilpech to spend the night.   During
the evening we had the pleasure of witnessing a native
dance.   As we approached we heard the noise of a drum,
and, upon entering the enclosure, found the men seated on
one side, and the women on the other. For some time there
was no dancing; but, after a while, a young man stood up in
the middle of the floor.   Another, with a handkerchief in
his hand having a knot tied in one end, walked along the
line of women and threw the handkerchief at one, after
doing which he returned to his seat.   This was considered
a challenge, and the woman rose, and, slowly taking her
shawl from her head, placed herself opposite the young
man, at a distance of about eight feet, and commenced dancing.   The dance was called the *toros*, or the bull.   The
performers occasionally changed places; when the tune
ended, the woman walked off.   The master of ceremonies,
called the *bastanero*, again walked along the line, and
touched another woman in the same way, and she also
danced with the young man for a time; and in this way
they continued, the dancing man being always the same,
and the partner being always provided for him.

Early next morning the party divided, two members
going north to visit Silam, and the balance, with the volan,
continuing toward the east, Tunkas being our objective
point, a village six leagues east of Sitilpech.   The road
for the first two miles was straight, level, stony, and unin-
teresting.   On both sides were low, thick woods, so that
there was no view except that of the road before us.   This,
however, soon changed, and the next few miles brought us

into a primeval forest of large trees, showing that beautiful, rich green foliage so characteristic of the tropics.   Here I first heard the notes of the parrot; they flew over our heads

in flocks of fifteen or twenty, uttering the most unearthly screams.   We fired into several flocks and secured half a dozen specimens.   They were the common green variety, but were very handsome specimens.

   We ate our dinner on the edge of a large *cenote*.   I was disappointed in not meeting with many birds here, for the locality seemed very favorable to their habits.   Occasionally we heard,

MEXICAN PARROT.

however, the long-drawn, wailing note of a jay somewhere in the adjacent woods; and, also, in the foliage edging the *cenote*, the noisy chattering of some small birds.   Another bird had a most sweet and melancholy song; it consisted simply of a few notes, uttered in a plaintive key, commenced high, and descended by harmonic intervals.   It was probably a species of warbler, but we were unable to identify it.   All these notes of birds were very striking, and characteristic of the forest.

   Late in the afternoon we again took up our line of march for Tunkas.   As we continued our walk the brief twilight commenced, and the sounds of multifarious life came from the vegetation around.   The whirring of cicadas; the shrill stridulation of a vast number and variety of field crickets and grasshoppers, each species sounding its peculiar note; the plaintive hooting of tree-frogs—all blended together in one continuous ringing sound,—the audible expression of the teeming profusion of nature.   As night came on, other species of animals joined the chorus.

   We arrived at Tunkas about 7:30 P. M.   This village was

of small size, containing but several hundred inhabitants. We succeeded in hiring a deserted hut, for the sum of one dollar a day, in which we swung our hammocks, and settled down for a few days' collecting. Our meals were taken in a grocery-store, and consisted of chocolate, black-beans (*frijolas*), tortillas, and beef.

Next morning we arose with the sun, shouldered our guns, and walked down a road which ran east from the vil-lage. Bird-life was here quite abundant, and we added largely to our collections. Among the insects we were especially interested in the Œcodoma, or leaf-cutting ant. This ant was seen everywhere about the suburbs, marching to and fro in broad columns. The habit of this ant of clip-ping and carrying away immense quantities of leaves has long been recorded in books of natural history. When em-ployed on this work, their processions look like a multitude of animated leaves on the march. In the course of my col-lecting, I had plenty of opportunities for observing them at work. They mount the trees in multitudes, the individuals being all workers. Each one places itself on the surface of a leaf, and cuts with its sharp, scissor-like jaws a nearly semi-circular incision on the upper side; it then takes the edge between its jaws, and by a sharp jerk detaches the piece. Sometimes they let the leaf drop to the ground, where a little heap accumulates, until carried off by another army of workers; but generally, each marches off with the piece it has operated upon, and all take the same road to their colony. It was a most interesting sight to see the vast host of busy workers occupied in this work. The leaves are used to thatch the domes which cover the entrances to their subterranean dwellings, thereby protecting from the deluging rains the young broods in the nests beneath. The nests of this ant are sometimes very extensive, being forty yards in circumference, but not more than two feet in

SKINNING BIRDS AT TUNKAS.

PLATE III.

height. It is very rarely that ants are seen at work on these mounds; the entrances seem to be generally closed; only now and then are the galleries opened.

The woods in the vicinity of Tunkas abound in various species of cacti, the most abundant form being that of the organ cactus, which grows to a height of from twenty to thirty feet. In one of these groves of cacti I first saw a trogan; it was seated alone on a branch, at no great elevation; a beautiful bird, with glossy back and rose-colored breast. The note of this handsome bird, uttered at intervals in a complaining tone, closely resembles the words "qua, qua." It is a dull, inactive bird, and does not readily take to flight when approached.

We spent three days in this interesting village, and added largely to our collections. Collecting, preparing our specimens, and making notes kept us well occupied. One day was so much like another that a description of each would be but a repetition. I was much interested one afternoon in the habits of a flock of blue jays; as I approached the flock, they flew across the road in a perfect string, presenting a fine shot.

The number and beauty of the birds did not equal our expectations. The majority we saw were small and obscurely colored; they were similar in general appearance to such as are met with in southern Florida. Occasionally a flock of parrots, green, with a patch of white on the forehead, would come at early morning to the trees near our hut. They would feed quietly, sometimes chattering in subdued tones, but setting up a harsh scream and flying off, on being disturbed. Humming-birds we did not see at this time, although we afterwards found them in the interior. Vultures we saw only at a distance, sweeping round at a great height over the village. The Mexican Goshawk (*Asturina plagiata*), was quite abundant. Flycatchers, finches, tanagers, and several other small birds, were quite abundant. Insects were more numerous in this neighbor-

hood than in any previously visited These were, however, mostly ants and beetles. But few species of butter-flies were seen, and these of a small, yellow variety.

As soon as night approached, swarms of goat-suckers made their appearance, wheeling about in a noise-less manner, in chase of night-flying insects. They sometimes descended and settled on the pathway, squatting down on their heels, and were then hard to distinguish from the surrounding soil. In the day-time they lay concealed in the woods, and venture forth only at night. They make no nest, but lay their eggs on the ground.

MEXICAN GOSHAWK.

March 4th we took our last ramble through this delight-ful region. The whole of the country for a score of miles was covered with an almost pathless forest, and there were but few roads which penetrated it. One road, in particular, I was very fond of following. The trees were large and many of them in bloom. This place was the resort of tan-agers, jays, groove-billed ani, and various species of hawks. Birds generally, however, were not numerous. The num-ber of butterflies, sporting about in this patch of woods on a sunny day, was so great as to give quite a character to the physiognomy of the place. It was impossible to walk far without disturbing flocks of them from the damp earth and pools of water left by the recent rains, where they congre-gated to imbibe the moisture. The most abundant were the sulphur-yellow and orange-colored varieties, which I started in swarms as I made my way along the road.

About 3 o'clock P. M. we hitched up the volan, and started on our return to Colonel Glenn's camp. Night overtook us while yet some miles east of Sitilpech, and we turned off on a side road which led to a hacienda, where we hoped to spend the night. The road, though smooth, was narrow, crooked, and dark. Occasionally a herd of cattle was seen, but they did not offer to molest us. Half a mile of this road brought us to a small, open space, in which was a native hut, built upon an elevation. Two or three dark-skinned children, with a man and woman, occupied the hut; on seeing us the man came out, and after hearing our wants, offered to let us have the use of an empty hut for the night, and also to give us a supper.

Here I first saw the *modus operandi* of preparing tortillas; they were made from maize, which was first soaked in water for some time. When they were ready to be fried, they were taken from the dish in which they had been soaking, and transferred to a large flat stone, called a *metate*, which was set at an angle like a washboard. A round stone, like a rolling pin, was then taken, and the corn was reduced to dough by a half-rolling, half grinding motion; they were then taken in small balls and patted with the hands into a thin cake, like our buckwheat cakes. They were fried on a flat, earthen dish, over a wood fire. The natives eat this with chile, but they have a very flat taste when eaten alone.

The native woman was thin and wrinkled, with sharp features, and, I should judge, a sharper tongue. The man was equally as wrinkled, but more amiable than his wife. Upon inquiring for the hut, we were shown a miserably dilapidated concern, but as it was the best we could do, we did not complain. We slung our hammocks, had a fire lighted to keep off the mosquitos, and prepared to spend the night as comfortably as possible. We suffered terribly, however, from insect pests; it was quite impossible to sleep on account of the mosquitos; they fell upon us by myriads, and without much noise came straight at cur faces. To add to our discomfort, the place was a perfect nest of fleas, and other pests too numerous to mention.

The day following we reached Sitilpech, and about noon of March 6th we reached Izamal, three miles from the camp. As we entered the town our eyes turned involuntarily to an immense mound rising grandly above the tops of the houses. It measured seven hundred feet long and sixty feet high. The whole of this structure was overgrown with trees and small shrubs, which aided us greatly in our ascent. The top of this mound commanded a grand view of level plains and undulating woodlands. This structure, like all those of Yucatan, was a truncated pyramid, terraced on one side, and descending perpendicularly to the ground on the opposite side. A wide and elaborate staircase once led to its summit, but this was now in ruins.

Opposite this mound, at a distance of a few yards, was another of lesser size, but containing a gigantic head cut in bas-relief. It was seven feet in height, and the same in width. The expression of the face was stern and repulsive.

On the north side of the plaza stood the church and convent of the Franciscan monks, on an elevation. Two flights of stone steps led up to it, opening upon an area fully two hundred feet square; on three sides of this square was a colonnade, forming a noble promenade, overlooking the town and surrounding country for a great distance. This elevation was probably artificial, and not the work of the Spaniards.

About 1 o'clock we again took up our line of march toward the camp, and arrived there three hours later, after suffering severely from the excessive heat. On the same

day the balance of the party arrived from Silam, they having ridden the whole distance in a volan in less than twelve
hours.

CHAPTER III.

DURING the three days spent at the camp, following our trip to Tunkas, we thoroughly explored the neighborhood and added very largely to our collections. One day was so much like another that I will refrain from a detailed account of each days' episodes.

The first thing that would strike a newcomer in the woods about the camp would be the apparant scarcity of birds; indeed, it often happened that we did not meet with a single bird during half a days' ramble in the most varied parts of the woods. Yet the country was tenanted by many hundred species, many of which were in reality abundant, and some of them conspicuous for their brilliant plumage. The cause of this apparent rarity was to be sought in the sameness of the forest which constituted their dwelling-place. The majority of the birds of the country were gregarious, at least during the season when they were most readily found; the fruit-eating species were to be met with only when certain wild fruits were ripe, and to know their exact localities required a great deal of experience.

While hunting along the narrow path-ways through the forest in the neighborhood of the camp, we would pass several hours without seeing many birds; but now and then the surrounding bushes and trees appeared suddenly to swarm with them. There were scores of birds, all moving about with the greatest activity—Crotophaga, woodpeckers, tanagers, flycatchers, and thrushes, flitting about the leaves and lower branches. The bustling crowd lost no time, but hurried along, each bird occupied on its account in scanning bark, leaf, or twig in search of insects. In a few minutes the host was gone, and the forest remained as silent as before. In the woods about the camp I witnessed quite frequently a curious case of protective resemblance; the Road-runners (*Geococcyx affinis*) when disturbed, would run along the top of the fences, or on the ground, keeping their wings close to their body and dropping their head to a level with the rest of their body, resembling so closely the iguanas that on several occasions I let them go thinking they were that animal.

Of the vertebrate animals we saw very little, except of lizards. They were sure to attract our attention by reason of their strange appearance, great numbers, and variety. The species which were seen crawling over the walls of the haciendas were different from those found in the forest. They were unpleasant looking animals, with colors assimilated to those of the stone walls and trees on which they were seen. A small species found near the haciendas was of speckled gray or ashy color. A slight rap would cause the tails of these lizards to snap off, the loss being partially repaired by a new growth.

Among the insects collected, the most interesting was the tarantula. These monstrous, heavy spiders, three or four inches in expanse, were found in many places about the camp. The different kinds had the most diversified habits. Some constructed dens of closely woven web among the tiles of thatch houses; others built similar nests in trees, while yet others built handsome nests in the ground, closing the aperture by a neatly constructed door. Several of the species were nocturnal in habit.

CYLINDRELLA
SPELUNCÆ, PFR.,
VAR. DUBIA,
PILSBRY.

It was a great disappointment to me that the mollusks were not more abundant; scarcely a living shell could be found. The cause of this paucity, so the Yucatecans informed me, lay in the dryness of the season, the wet season being the most favorable for Molluscan, as well as for insect life. I found, however, numerous specimens of the genera Glandina, Cyclotus, Cylindrella, and Choanopoma.

Early on the morning of the 10th, we packed up our specimens and left the Colonel's camp for Merida; the Colonel and Mrs. Glenn accompanied us. From Merida we took the *Ferro carril de Merida c' Calkini* for Santa Cruz, situated in the nortwestern part of Yucatan. Here we were met by three volans which conveyed us to the hacienda of Señor Escalente, where we expected to add very largely to our collections, and also to visit a famous limestone cave.

Our nine mile ride was most interesting. The drivers whipped the mules into a gallop, and kept it up throughout the entire journey. To urge the mules he uttered the words " moola, moola! " at the same time clucking loudly with his lips. As we approached the hacienda, cultivated fields of henequen appeared on either side, stretching away in the distance as far as the eye could reach   A turn in the road brought us in sight of the hacienda, and with a rush we galloped through the open gateway into the courtyard, and drew up at the foot of a broad flight of steps. This was one of the finest estates in Yucatan, employing several hundred natives about the place. In addition to the hacienda building there were huts, cattle-yards, and a church enclosed by a high stone wall. Here were native men and women passing to and fro through the court, each busy with his or her daily task. The henequen machines were busy preparing the henequen for shipment, and everything had an air of business which was quite new to us.

The major-domo received us, Señor Escalente being ill, and extended to us the hospitalities of the house. In a short time a savory supper was prepared, to which we did full justice. At sunset we heard the bells of the chapel sounding the *oracion*, or evening prayer, and the natives gathered around with uncovered heads. When it was finished, they gave us, and each other, the salutation of " *Buenas noches* " before retiring. This was a beautiful and impressive custom, which we observed throughout our travels in Yucatan. The cold was so intense during the night that I awoke several times actually suffering from its effects. During the day the sun beats down upon the earth with intense force. The rapid radiation at night sometimes produces cold intense enough to cause water to freeze.

In the morning, after a refreshing bath, we shouldered our guns, insect boxes, and pouches, and walked into the woods covering the north side of the Sierra. On our way we saw numbers of swallows, flycatchers, and hawks. Their shrill cry was often heard, with now and then the loud tapping of a woodpecker. We were not successful in shooting, and in about an hour were joined by the rest of the party on horseback, on their way across the Sierra to visit the large cave of which I spoke before. After passing the summit of the Sierra, we descended twenty feet or more to the mouth of the cave.

This was in the form of a circular well, thirty feet in diameter and twenty in depth; descending this we found ourselves in a circular chamber, from which numerous passages branched to right and left. At one corner was a rude natural opening in a great mass of limestone rock, low and narrow, through which rushed a powerful current of air, agitating the branches and leaves in the immediate vicinity. At the distance of a few feet the descent was precipitous, and we went down by a ladder about twenty feet. Here all light from the mouth of the well was lost; but we soon reached the brink of a very steep descent, to the bottom of which a strong body of light was thrown from a hole in the surface, a perpendicular depth, as we afterward learned, of one hundred and ten feet. As we stood on the brink of this precipitous path, under the immense shelving mass of rock, seeming darker from the stream of light thrown down the hole, gigantic stalactites and larger blocks of stone as-

sumed all manner of fantastic shapes, and seemed like the
bodies of monstrous animals.   From this passage others
branched off to right and left.   Beyond the circular opening we passed into a large vaulted chamber of stone,
with a high roof supported by enormous stalactitic pillars.
Farther on we climbed up a high, broken piece of rock, and
descended again by a low, narrow opening, through which
we were obliged to crawl, and which, from its closeness,
and the heat and labor of crawling through it, made us pant
with exhaustion.   This brought us to a rugged, perpendicular hole, three or four feet in diameter, with steps barely
large enough for a foothold, worn in the rock.   The passage here descended rapidly, and we were again obliged to
stoop to avoid knocking our heads against the roof of the
passage.   It then enlarged into a rather spacious cavern,
which was filled with gigantic stalactitic columns.   Here
our journey in this direction ended.   Several passageways
led from this chamber, but they had not been explored, and
the guides would not attempt their exploration.   What lay
beyond no one knew.   Leaving this chamber we returned
to the circular well near the mouth of the cave, and explored
a long passage leading in a northerly direction.   This was
found to descend rapidly for three or four hundred feet, and
then to end in a shelving point.   The greatest depth of this
cave was 180 feet, and the longest passage explored by us
one eighth of a mile.   The whole range of hills was composed of transition, or mountain limestone, and was said
to contain many such caves as the one we had just visited.
Swallows (*Stelgidopteryx serripennis*) were seen flying about
the outer chamber of the cave in great numbers, and seemed
to be constructing nests on the rugged face of the walls.
The view from the summit of the Sierra was very picturesque;
away to the south could be seen two parallel ranges of
mountains, the intervening spaces being well wooded.   To

the north lay the buildings composing the hacienda, concealed among a grove of palms and ceiba trees.

In the afternoon we visited several newly constructed wells for geological information. On the road we saw a number of huge mounds, but as our time was limited we did not stop to examine them. In the evening, at sunset, the scene was lovely. The groups of tall palms, the large ceiba trees relieved against the golden sky, the native huts surrounded with trees, and the background of dense forest, all softened by the mellowed light of the magical half-hour after sunset, formed a picture indescribably beautiful.

On the 12th we returned to Merida, and from thence took the Merida and Peto railroad for Ticul. On our way to Merida from Santa Cruz, the railroad officials allowed us the unusual privilege of having the train stopped wherever we wished to study a good cut. And all this for science! On our way to Ticul we were delayed several hours by a derailed tender. Arriving at Ticul we were received by Señor Fajada, and given rooms in his mercantile house for our use during our stay. We took our meals at a café near the plaza.

The town of Ticul was worthy the visit of any of our European travellers. The first time I looked upon it from the roof of the convent, it struck me as the perfect picture of stillness and repose. The plaza was overgrown with grass; a few mules were pasturing upon it, and now and then a single horseman crossed it. The roof of the convent was on a level with, or above, the tops of the houses, and the view was of a great plain, with houses of one story, flat roofs, high garden walls, above which orange, lemon, and plantain trees were growing, and the only noise was the singing of the birds. All business was done early in the morning or toward evening, and through the rest of the day, during the heat, the inhabitants were within doors, and it might almost have passed for a deserted town.

Like all Mexican towns, it was laid out with its plaza and streets running at right angles, and was distinguished among the towns of Yucatan for its stone houses. These were on the plaza and streets adjoining; outside these, and extending more than a mile each way, were the huts of the natives. These huts were generally plastered, enclosed by stone fences, and overgrown and concealed by weeds. The population was said to be about ten thousand, of which about a thousand were white people, and the rest natives.

The church and convent occupied the whole of one side of the plaza. Both were built by the Franciscan monks, and they were among the grandest of those buildings with which that wonderful order marked its entrance into the country. They stood on a stone platform about four feet high and several hundred feet in front. The church was large and sombre, and adorned with rude monuments and figures calculated to inspire the ignorant natives with awe. The convent was connected with the church by a spacious corridor, now much in ruins. It was a large structure built of stone, with massive walls, and four hundred feet in length. The entrance was under a wide portico, with stone pillars, from which ascended a broad flight of steps to a spacious corridor twenty feet wide. This corridor ran through the whole length of the building, with a stone pavement, and was lighted from the roof which had fallen in. Everything about the old convent bespoke ruin and decay.

CHAPTER IV.

On the morning following our arrival in Ticul, Señor Fajada provided three volans, with drivers, to convey us to the ruins of Uxmal. We left Ticul about 7 o'clock, passing through the southern portion of the town, which was composed of native huts. As we sped along, the inhabitants came out to look at us. The town was soon left behind, and we entered the scrubbily-wooded portion of the country. Our road ran along the base of the Sierra for several leagues, but finally turned north and crossed the range of hills at an elevation of about two hundred and twenty-five feet. We passed several haciendas, at one of which we stopped for water. Here we shot our first humming-birds (*Lampornis Prevosti*). Flycatchers and grackles were very common, and several small warblers were seen, but we had not time enough to procure them.

The ascent of the Sierra was steep, broken, and stony; the whole range was a mass of limestone rock, with a few stunted trees, not numerous enough to afford shade, and white under the reflection of the sun. In three-quarters of an hour we reached the top. Looking back, our last view of the plain presented a long stretch of scantily-wooded, level country, and high above everything else a group of cocoa-palms near a large hacienda. The only people we met was a hunting party of natives, who had shot a young doe. About 11 o'clock we reached the Hacienda of Uxmal (pronounced Ush-mahl).

This hacienda stood in the midst of the plain, with its cattle-yard, tanks, and cieba trees. Stopping but a few minutes, to procure a guide for the ruins, we continued on our journey, and in fifteen minutes, emerging from the

woods, came out upon a field in which stood a large
mound surmounted by a ruined building—the House of the
Dwarf, or *Casa del Adivino*.   The sides of this lofty structure were covered with high grass, bushes, and small trees,
twenty or more feet high.   The mound fronted a courtyard measuring one hundred and thirty feet by eighty-five.
The mound itself measured two hundred and thirty-five
feet in length, and one hundred and fifty-five in width.   It
was about eighty-eight feet in height, and one hundred feet
to the top of the building on its summit.   It was not a true

pyramid in form, for its ends were rounded. It was encased
in stone, and appeared to rise solid from the plain.   At a
height of sixty feet was a projecting platform, on which
stood a building loaded with ornaments, which we afterwards found were more rich and varied than those of any
other building in the ruins.   A great doorway opened upon
the platform; inside this aperture were two chambers; the
outer one fifteen feet wide, seven feet deep, and nineteen
feet high, and the inner one twelve feet wide, four feet deep,
and eleven feet high.   Both were plain, without ornament
of any kind.

The steps leading to the building were all in ruins,
and it was dangerous to ascend them.   The crown-

ing structure of this mound was a long and narrow building, measuring fully seventy feet in length by twelve in
depth. The front was much ruined, but enough was intact
to show that it must have been elaborately ornamented.
The interior was divided into three apartments of nearly
equal size. What was very curious was the fact that none
of these apartments had any communication with each
other. Two doors opened to the east and one to the west.
On the eastern front there was a grand stair-case over a
hundred feet high, half again as wide, and containing some
eighty or ninety steps, now very much in ruins. This
mound, and the building on its summit, was used by the
ancient Mayas as a Teocalli, or temple, and upon it they
offered up their human sacrifices. The view from this
height was grand, taking in the whole field of ruins.

Looking from the House of the Dwarf, the first building to catch the eye was the *Casa del Gobernador*, or House
of the Governor, built upon several terraces. This was
the largest building among the ruins, and measured three
hundred and twenty feet in length. A portion of the right-
hand side of the face of the building had fallen, and now
lay in a mass of ruins. The left-hand side was more perfect, and we could see that the building must have been
elaborately ornamented, and must, indeed, have been a
grand sight when entire. The building was constructed
entirely of stone; up to the cornice, which ran entirely
around, the façade presented a solid mass of ornamentation. One ornament which was very conspicuous, and
which attracted our eye at once, was over the center doorway, and while very much in ruins, yet enough of it was
left for us to make out its general character. It represented
a figure seated upon a throne, which must have been supported by an ornament of some kind, but which had now
fallen. The head-dress was lofty, and from it proceeded

plumes which fell symmetrically on each side, and touched
the ornament on which the feet of the figure rested.

Another ornament which was seen about the ruins
more frequently than any other, consisted of a stone pro·
jecting from the wall one foot and seven inches, and in the

ROOM IN THE HOUSE OF THE GOVERNOR.

shape of a coiled elephant's trunk. This projecting stone
was seen in many places about the building, and especially
on the corners.   It was always associated with, and
formed part of another, consisting of scroll work and
squares, and was probably intended to convey some idea,
either historical or mythical, to the people who inhabited
this city.   In fact, everything about these ornaments
seemed to point to the fact that they were hieroglyphics,
intended to represent the history of these strange people.

The rear elevation of this building was a solid wall,
without doorways or openings of any kind.   The two ends

were thirty-nine feet deep, and had each a single doorway. The sculptured ornaments were very much simpler on the ends and rear than those in front. The roof was flat and was originally cemented, but the cement had become broken, and the whole was now covered with a mass of vegetation. There were eleven doorways in front and one at each end. The doors were all gone, and the wooden lintels had rotted away and fallen. In front and in the center were grand flights of steps ascending the three terraces, but they were in a ruinous condition.

The interior was divided longitudinally by a wall into two corridors, and these again, by cross partitions, into oblong rooms. These rooms communicated with the exterior by doorways, the inner one being exactly opposite the outer one. The floor was of cement, in many places broken, and covered all over with fallen débris from the ceiling and walls.

The terraces upon which stood the *Casa del Gobernador* were very interesting, and a description of the building would not be complete without a description also of these terraces. The lowest was three feet high, fifteen feet broad (it formed part of a shelving mound), and five hundred and seventy-five feet long; the second was twenty feet high, two hundred and fifty feet wide, and five hundred and forty-five feet in length; the third was nineteen feet high, thirty feet broad, and three hundred and sixty feet long. The second terrace was still in a good state of preservation, but the others were more or less in ruins. The whole was covered with a rank growth of bushes, weeds, and small trees, so we were not able to well make out all the characters.

To the left of the House of the Governor rose a gigantic mound, sixty-five feet in height, and three hundred at the base. Its sides were covered with a rank growth of vegetation, which helped not a little in its ascent. On the top was a great platform of solid stone, seventy-five feet square; fifteen feet from the top was a narrow terrace running around on the four sides. The corners once bore sculptured ornaments, but the remains were now all that was visible. In one side of the mound, at the narrow terrace before spoken of, was a small chamber about four feet square, but aside from this not a hole was to be seen. From the summit a grand view could be had, showing a well wooded plain in the distance, and the ruined city lying at its base.

In a line directly north of this mound was another large building—the *Casa de las Monjas,* or House of the Nuns. This building was quadrangular, with a courtyard in the center. It stood on the higher of three terraces; it was two hundred and seventy-nine feet long, and above the cornice, from one end to the other, was ornamented with sculpture. In the center was a gateway ten feet wide, leading to the courtyard. On each side of this gateway were four doorways, opening to apartments twenty-four feet wide and seventeen feet high; these rooms had no communication with each other. The building that formed the right or eastern side of the quadrangle was one hundred and fifty-eight feet long; that on the left was one hundred and seventy-three feet long, and the range of buildings opposite, or at the end of the quadrangle, measured two hundred and sixty-four feet. These three ranges of buildings had no doorways on the outside, but the interior of each was a blank wall, and above the cornice all were ornamented with rich sculpture. The courtyard upon which these four buildings faced was two hundred and fourteen feet wide, and two hundred and fifty-eight feet deep. The first building spoken of contained sixteen rooms, in two rows of eight, the outside not opening upon the courtyard. The face of this building was covered with the most elaborately sculptured ornaments, most conspicuous among which were two colossal serpents entwined, which encompassed nearly all the other ornaments. The other two buildings were about the same size, and almost equally as rich in ornamentation. Fronting the entrance gate was a lofty building, two hundred and sixty-four feet long, standing on a terrace twenty feet high. It was ascended by a grand staircase ninety-five feet wide, flanked on each side by a building with sculptured front, and having three doorways, each leading to an apartment.

The height of this building to the upper cornice was twenty-five feet. It had thirteen doorways, over each of which rose a perpendicular wall ten feet wide and seventeen feet high, above the cornice. The stair-case was very much in ruins, as indeed were all the buildings. In one of the wings of this building was seen the curious Maya arch, built without a keystone.

THE MAYA ARCH.

Near the *Casa de las Monjas* was another building, the *Casa de las Tortugas*, or House of the Turtles, but it was in such a state of ruin that a description was impossible. Away to the southwest lay the range of ruined walls known as the *Casa de Palomos*, or House of the Pigeons. It was two hundred and forty feet long; the front was very much in ruins, and the apartments filled with the fallen débris. On the roof, running longitudinally along its center, was a range of structures built in pyramidal form, re-sembling some of the old Dutch houses. These were originally nine in number, built of stone, about three feet thick, and had small oblong openings through them. It was from these holes, resembling pigeon houses, that the building derived its name. The names of all the buildings were misnomers, given by the Spanish residents and not by the natives. This building was very much in ruins, but enough remained to show that it once contained a large courtyard in its center. Several other ruined buildings lay buried among the underbrush, but they were in such a fallen condition that it was useless to make a study of them.

Such was Uxmal, one of the most interesting of the ruins of Central America. Ruin and decay have been steadily at work, and before many years have passed, this famous relic of the ancient Mayas will be a thing of the past. Over all the buildings a rank vegetation is struggling for the mastery, and the end is inevitable. Uxmal is probably better known to the general public than any other of the Yucatan ruins, on account of the published writings of Stevens, LePlongeon, Charnay, Norman, Waldeck, and others. It was with many regrets that we entered our volans, and saw the ruined city disappear from our view.

Animal life was remarkably rare about the ruins. A few bats, insects, dead mollusks, and occasionally a fly-catcher, were all we saw. It is quite possible that during the rainy season, life is much more abundant.

Lunch was taken at the Hacienda of Uxmal. Here I saw many sculptured figures which had been taken from the ruins. Among others was a large sculptured ornament, representing a double headed lynx, with the bodies joined together in the middle. It was carved from one piece of stone, and must have been a tremendous undertaking. The sculpture, however, was rude and uncouth, as were all the ornaments at Uxmal.

At four o'clock we again entered our volans and started for Ticul, arriving there late in the evening. Our ride over the Sierra was something of an experience, for we went galloping down the steep slopes, the volan swaying from side to side in a way most alarming to weak nerves. A very noticeable feature of Yucatan evenings was the silence which seemed to reign supreme over the woods. Hardly a sound could be heard, save the clatter of the volan, the voice of the driver as he urged the mules, or the occasional cry of some wild animal.

On the following morning we again set forth, this time to visit the Hacienda of Tabi, owned by Señor Fajada, and also to visit a large cave and the ruins of Labná. Our road was very rough and rocky, and bordered by dense woods. At eleven o'clock we came to the clearing in which was situated the Hacienda of Tabi. It was a noble building of good proportions, built of stone, and of two stories. The cattle-yard was large, shaded by fine ramon trees (a species of tropical oak), with here and there a towering cocoa-palm, and filled by a large herd of cattle. I have already given the reader some idea of a hacienda in Yucatan, with its cattle-yards, its great tanks of water, and other accessories. All these were upon a large scale, equal to any we had seen. Besides the hacienda building, native huts, etc., there was a rum distillery and sugar refinery, from both of which Señor Fajada derived an immense revenue   For the safety of the hacienda against the marauding natives of the interior, there was a company of soldiers stationed here. About the cocoa-palms in the cattle-yard large flocks of grackles were flying; these birds seemed always to congregate about haciendas, but were never found in the forests.   In one portion of the cattle-yard I discovered a small land snail which proved to be a new species (*Oryzosoma Tabiensis, Pilsbry*). At dinner I tasted a dish of which I had heard much, but until this time had not tasted—cuttle-fish. It was a small species of Octopus found abundantly on the coast, and was very palatable, tasting much like chicken.

ORYZOSOMA
TABIENSIS,
PILSBRY.

Early in the afternoon we started for the Cave of Loltun, situated a league from the hacienda. The road for the

distance of two miles was level, and bordered fields of henequen; it then ascended at a moderate angle until we reached
an abrupt opening, circular in outline, fully sixty feet in circumference, seeming a magnificent entrance to a great temple for the worsh p of the god of nature. We first descended by a succession of short ladders laid against the face
of the wall of the cavern, and entered a large, vaulted cavern
about sixty feet in height, lighted from the mouth.   In this
chamber were many weird and gigantic stalactites incrusted
with the disintegrated earth, which gave them a brownish
tinge. From here we entered a second chamber about twenty
feet below, in which was a most beautiful display of stalactitic
growth; here were gigantic columns of pure, white calcite,
reaching from the floor to the roof above. We had been
told of numerous figures and objects of domestic utensils
used by the ancient inhabitants, which were to be found in
this cave, but as was most usually the case we were doomed
to disappointment, for the so called figures were nothing
more than the huge stalactitic columns before us.

From this chamber we journeyed on by a downward,
shelving path, and entered another of surpassing weirdness;
it was fully three hundred feet in diameter, and lighted from
a circular hole in the roof, eighty feet above, through which
streamed the sunlight. At one end of this large chamber
was a smaller one, about as large as a good sized room.
Against the wall of this apartment was a most delicious
fountain of clear, cold water, bubbling up from a hollow stal-
agmite. When emptied of its contents this fountain slowly
filled again, but did not run over. The exact temperature
we were, unfortunately, not able to determine.

From this small chamber several dark passages
branched to right and left, but they had not been explored,
and the guides would not enter them. Recrossing the
large cavern we entered a dark passage, fifty feet in height,

which led to a huge cavern strewn with broken rocks which had fallen from the roof above. For the space of twenty minutes we clambered over these boulders, and finally reached a level path in a passage some fifteen or twenty feet high and twenty-five in width. The floor was broken into ripple-marks, like those on a sea-shore, and looked as though water had flowed over it at some distant day. This path was followed for some distance, when it branched in several directions; one branch led straight ahead and was said to lead to a small village some six miles away, and was used by the ancient Mayas as a place of retreat when hard pressed by their enemies. The other passages led through a labyrinth of stalactitic columns, and we did not explore them. As evening was approaching, we returned to the hacienda.

This cave was but one of many such which are scattered throughout Yucatan. The whole surface of the country is flat and without a water course of any kind, so that the inhabitants are compelled to depend upon the water obtained in cenotes, caves, and tanks for their supply. There are numerous streams throughout the country in the depths of these caves; one notable instance is the Cave of Bolonchen, in which, at the depth of some four hundred feet, a stream of good water is found. This is probably true of all the caves, although some have not yet been explored sufficiently to determine whether all are thus supplied or not. As the country is composed of transition limestone it is natural that numerous caves should abound, and that the water should seek its lowest level in the softest rock.

CHAPTER V.

THE next morning we set out for the ruins of Labná. Our road lay southeast, among the hills, and was very picturesque. A damp fog hung over everything, and the air was quite cold. It was in fact a most dismal day.

A VOLAN COCHE.

At the distance of two leagues we reached a field of ruins hidden in the dense forest. The first building we saw was the most curious and extraordinary structure we had yet seen, surmounting a pyramidal mound forty-five feet high. The steps had fallen, and trees and Maguey plants were growing out of the place where they had stood. A narrow platform formed the top of the mound. The building faced the south, and when entire measured forty-three feet in front and twenty feet in width. It had three doorways, of which one, together with ten feet of the whole structure, had fallen, and now lay a mass of ruins. The center doorway opened into two chambers, each twenty feet long and six feet wide.

Above the cornice of the building rose a gigantic perpendicular wall thirty feet high, which had once been ornamented from one side to the other with colossal figures, now broken and in fragments, but still presenting a curious appearance. Along the top, standing out on the wall, was a row of deaths' heads; underneath were two lines of human figures in alto relievo. Over the center doorway was a colossal seated figure, of which only detached portions now remained. The wall was tottering and ready to fall, and a crack had already separated the remaining portion; it is only a question of a few years when the whole of this wonderful building will be a mere shapeless mound.

At the distance of a few hundred feet from this structure was an arched gateway, remarkably beautiful in its proportions and grace of ornament. On the right, running off at an angle of thirty-five degrees, was a long building much in ruins. On the left it formed an angle with another building. The gateway was ten feet wide, and fifteen feet high, passing through which we entered a spacious

RUINED BUILDING.

courtyard overgrown with weeds and small trees. The doors of the apartments on both sides of the gateway, each twelve feet by eight, opened upon this area. Above the cornice, the face of the building was rich in sculpture. The buildings around the courtyard formed a great irregular pile, measuring in all two hundred feet in length.

Northeast from the mound on which stood the great wall, and about one hundred and sixty yards distant, was a large building, erected on a terrace, and hidden among the trees growing upon it, with its front much ruined. Still further in the same direction was another large building of really magnificent proportions. It stood on a large terrace, four hundred feet long and one hundred and fifty feet deep. The whole terrace was covered with buildings. The front of the building measured two hundred and eighty feet in length. It consisted of three distinct parts, differing very much in style. The whole long façade was ornamented with sculptured stone, of good workmanship. On the left end of the principal building, in the angle of the corner, was the most curious and elaborate ornament we had as yet seen. It represented the open jaws of an alligator, enclosing a human head.

In the platform in front of the buildings were several circular holes leading to subterranean chambers, dome-shaped, eleven feet long, seven wide and ten high, to the center of the arch. These chambers were probably used as storehouses for maize. As we observed at Uxmal, the façade below the cornice was of plain stone without ornamentation of any kind, while above it was covered with sculptured stones. There were about twenty doors facing the front, and the rear elevation was perfectly blank. Above this building, and built upon its roof, was a second, much smaller, with an elaborately sculptured façade. This building was divided into several rooms. The doors here had an addition, not before observed in any building in Uxmal; this was two pillars of stone dividing the doorway into three apertures. This character was not observed in the buildings below. The roof was much fallen and overgrown with large and small trees, which were running their roots into the crevices among the stones, and slowly but surely causing the ruin of these interesting relics of by-gone days.

In the interest of our work, I had not discovered that thousands of garrapatas were crawling over me. These insects are the scourge of Yucatan, and altogether were a more constant source of annoyance and suffering than any we encountered in the country. These, in color, size, and numbers, were like grains of sand, and dispersed themselves all over my body, getting into the seams of my clothes, and burying themselves in my flesh. Their habit was to attach

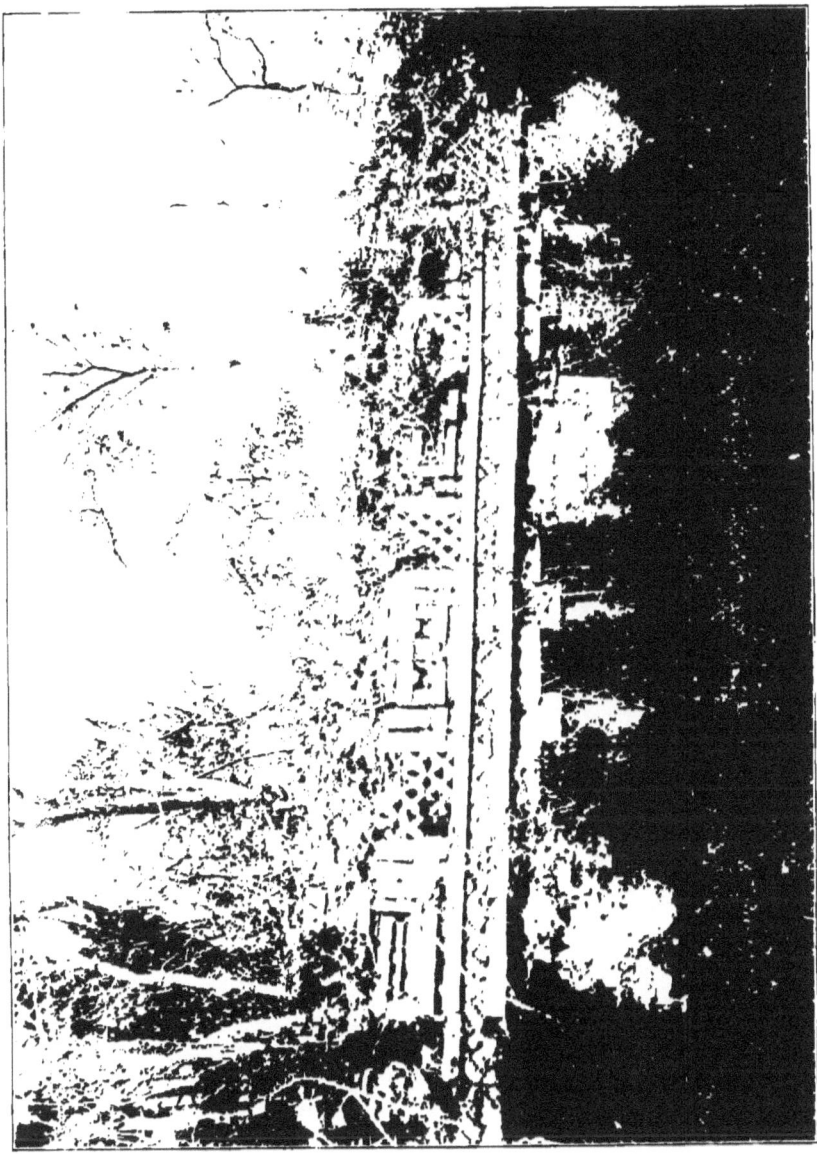

RUINS OF LABNA.

PLATE IV

themselves to the skin by plunging their proboscis into it, and thus suck the blood until their flat bodies were distended into a globular form.

It was very curious that so few birds were seen about the ruins. Among those observed were the Guatemalan Woodpecker, Uxmal Woodpecker, Ruby-throated Hummingbird, Mexican Kingbird, and a single specimen, which we obtained, of Gray's Thrush. *Glandina Cylindracœ*, one of the most abundant mollusks of Yucatan, was found here in considerable numbers. Another abundant species was the *Chondropoma Largillierti*, a beautiful yellowish-white shell with rows of brown spots. *Bulimulus tropicalis* and *Cyclotus Dysoni*, a beautiful ribbed species, and a *Helicina*, were the common forms seen. One new variety of *Cylindrella* was found (*C. speluncœ, var. dubia*). A single snake (*Dryophis fulgidus*) was seen and captured. A rabbit was also seen, but not obtained. Insects were not seen (excepting the troublesome garrapatas).

It was with much regret that we left the region without visiting the other ruined cities of the country—Chichen Itza, Xampon, Kabah, Chunhuhu, etc.—and comparing their architecture with that of Uxmal and Labná. The predominating character, however, was that they were all built upon artificial pyramids or terraces. A truncated pyramid supported a building of greater or lesser dimensions. The walls were very thick, many of them faced on the interior with carved stones, and presenting richly sculptured façades, sculptured in bas-relief. Human heads, figures of men and animals, and hieroglyphics consisting of squares, scrolls, and other geometric figures, constituted the principal ornamentation. Although these ruins have been studied by the most famous archæologists of the present century, yet little is known concerning their history. A short stop was made at the Hacienda of Tabi, and then we started for Ticul, arriving there shortly after dark.

During our two days sojourn in Ticul, we added largely to our collections. Here I was, unfortunately, laid up with fever and not able to do much collecting. While preparing insects or skinning birds in the house, the window which opened into the courtyard was generally filled with men and boys, who would wait for hours, watching our operations with the most untiring curiosity. They would whisper among themselves, and as we dexterously removed a skin, they would give exclamations of wonder. And then they would guess as to what we were going to do with them; some thought they were to show, and others that we used them as medicine.

Our stay in Ticul was marred by my sickness, having been seized the second day with an attack of dysentery, which confined me to my hammock for some time. The balance of the party, however, did good work, and added largely to our collections. During my indisposition I took my meals, when strong enough, in a café near the plaza. Nothing but Spanish was spoken, of course, and at every meal the following dialogue took place. It is a fair sample of the restaurant conversation between native and foreigner:

Tiene Vd. pan?	Have you bread.
Si, Senor.	Yes, sir.
Y huevos fretos?	And fried eggs?
Si, Senor.	Yes, sir.
Y cafe?	And coffee?
Si, Senor.	Yes, sir.
Y carne frio?	And cold meat?
Si, Senor.	Yes, sir.
Traigame Vd. todo.	Bring me all.
Si, Senor.	Yes, sir.

Our explorations in this direction were productive of good results, so far as the avifauna was concerned. The Mexican Ground Dove was very common about the towns and haciendas. The Aztec Paroquet was seen in small flocks about the mountains near Ticul. The Groove-billed Ani, or Crotophaga, was everywhere abundant. After dark, on the roads, the Parauque was seen frequently. The little Cinnamon Humming-bird was quite common in the suburbs of Ticul. The Least Fly-catcher, Yellow-bellied Green Jay, and Great-tailed Grackle were quite common. The Yucatan Cardinal was one of the most beautiful and conspicuous birds. At Ticul it was commonly seen about the slopes of the mountains. Among the smaller birds, the following were seen and many captured: White-eyed Vireo, Parula Warbler, Sycamore Warbler, Black-throated Green Warbler, Yucatan Mockingbird, and Blue-Gray Gnatcatcher. Many of these small birds were seen feeding on the berries of the Palmetto trees.

Gray's Thrush (*Merula grayi*) was seen about Ticul, but none captured at that place. One was shot by Mr. Stone at Labná. Our visit occurred during the dry season, and was not the best for ornithological purposes. Later in the season, we were told, occurs a migration of birds north-ward, and at that time they are much more numerous, both in species and individuals.

On the 18th we left Ticul for Merida. The road between Ticul and Merida bordered large tracts of ground, in which henequen and corn were being cultivated. The system of agriculture in Yucatan is rather primative. Besides hemp and sugar, the principal products of the country are corn, beans, and calabazas, like our pumpkins and squashes, camotes, like our potatoes, and chile or pepper, of which last an enormous quantity is consumed, both by native and Spaniard. Indian corn, however, is the great staple, and the cultivation of this probably differs but little from the system followed by the natives before the conquest. In the dry season, generally in the months of January and

February, a place is selected in the woods, from which the trees are cut down and burned.   In May or June the corn is planted.   This is done by making little holes in the ground with a pointed stick, putting in a few grains of corn and covering them over.   Once in the ground, it is left to take care of itself   The corn has a fair start with the weeds, and thus keep pace together.   The hoe and plough are here unknown; indeed, the plough could be of but little use here on account of the stony nature of the ground; the machete, a long, hatchet-like knife, is the only instrument employed.

While in Merida we called upon the American Consul, Mr. Thompson, who is a most enthusiastic archæologist. He had himself discovered upwards of forty ruinèd cities, before unknown.   He had accumulated quite a collection of hatchets, vases, birds, and other relics found about the ruins. What was of the greatest interest to me was his superb collection of photographs, numbering many hundred, of all the large ruins.*   From him we learned that during the wet season, animal life is very abundant, and many species of birds are found which do not live here in the dry season.

At three o'clock in the afternoon we left Merida for Progreso, there to spend a few days before leaving the country for Veracruz.   Col. Glenn and his wife left us at Merida, to return to the construction camp.   During the evening, we all enjoyed a much needed bath in the waters of the Gulf.

The next four days we spent in collecting, and as birdlife was very abundant, we added considerably to our already full collections.   Back of the town was a broad lagoon inhabited by many species of aquatic birds.   Flocks of gulls were seen flying overhead, uttering their well-known cry, and herons of several species wading about the swampy portion. The land bordering the Gulf was sandy and covered with a

*NOTE.—The ruins of Yucatan in front of the Anthropological Building of the World's Columbian Exposition, were the work of this gentleman.

growth of low, thorny bushes, interspersed with tall cocoa-palms. In this scrubby portion we shot a number of very interesting specimens. The little Cactus Wren was very abundant, constantly on the move among the bushes, and very difficult to shoot. We frequently saw the Man-o-War Bird flying several hundred yards off shore, but although we fired at them constantly, we were not able to shoot one. In the mangroves bordering the lagoon we found numerous small birds, among them a number of flycatchers. These birds were the most abundant in Yucatan, both in species and individuals. About the edges of the mangroves the White-rumped Swallow, Great Blue Heron, Killdeer Plover, White Egret, and Louisiana Heron were quite abundant; the Blue-winged Teal was often seen, but not in any numbers. The Kingbird was not uncommon. Of this bird (*Tyrannus melancholicus*) we obtained three specimens. The same species (apparently) was seen in the interior, although but one specimen was shot in the latter region, and that differed in some respects from the Progreso specimens. The Progreso specimens are much lighter beneath and contain much less red in the crest, than in the inland bird.

We spent most of our afternoons and evenings in wandering up and down the beach, picking up the specimens which had been thrown up by the last tide.

During our stay, I observed the habits of many of the common marine animals. Among others, a large sea-slug (*Aplysia*) was very common. This mollusk is about five inches long; of a dirty yellowish color, veined with purple. It feeds on the delicate sea-weeds which grow among the stones in shallow water. When disturbed, this slug emits a fine purplish-red fluid, which stains the water for some distance. These harmless creatures were once supposed to be poisonous, on account of this purple fluid.

In many places the beach was fairly heaped with dead

shells, while in others it was nearly clean, being one vast extent of smooth, glistening sand. I enumerated about fifty species, mostly confined to the class Gastropoda. The Pelecypods were few in species, but numerous in individuals, more so in fact than the Gastropods. Of the predominating genera I noted the following: *Fulgur, Crepidula, Columbella, Fasciolaria, Strombus, Olivella, Venus, Arca, Pinna*, and *Ostrea. Venus cancellata* was very common and of extreme interest, as it is found fossil throughout the interior. The little *Olivella mutica* was as common as on the first day we hunted for it, four weeks ago. By the side of an old, wrecked hull of a schooner, I found a heap of shells in which I reaped my greatest harvest. Inside the old schooner I found a colony of *Melampas* (*M. coffeus*), from which I collected a dozen or more specimens.

This abundance of material indicated a rich zoological province off the Yucatan banks, and this indication has been proven correct by the dredgings of the United States Fish, Coast and Geodetic Survey Steamer "Blake" in the last fifteen years.

On the afternoon of the 22d, we left Progreso and embarked on the City of Alexandria, which was to sail next day for Veracruz. A word in relation to the derivation of the word Yucatan, before we leave the country. It is supposed by some to have been derived from the plant known as *Yuca*, and *thale*, the heap of earth in which this plant grows; the most general belief is that it is derived from certain words spoken by the natives in answer to the question: "What is the name of this country?" and the answer, "I do not understand your words," which expression, in the language of the natives, has some resemblance to the pronounciation of the word Yucatan. The natives have never recognized the name, however, and to this day, among themselves, they speak of their country only under the ancient name of Maya, and call themselves a Macegual instead of a Yucateco.

Before leaving Yucatan, a few words in regard to its civilization may not be deemed inappropriate. The population numbers about 500,000, and is mostly native. Besides its churches, convents, and public buildings, it has thirteen newspapers, several electric light plants, telephone exchange, street cars, and six lines of railway, viz: two lines from Merida to Progreso, one narrow and the other wide guage; a line from Merida to Ticul, one from Merida to Peto, one from Merida to Calkini, and one from Merida to Sotuta. There are also in the state eight cities, fifteen towns, one hundred and fifty villages, three hundred and fifty haciendas, and over one hundred ruined cities, besides numerous abandoned settlements.

Late on the afternoon of the 23rd, we left Progreso for Veracruz. Our trip across the Gulf was without any notable event. During the evenings, which we spent on deck, we were interested in studying the phosphorescence which could be plainly seen as the vessel sped along. This was caused by myriads of little animals, whose bodies gave off the silvery light. Chief among these animals were the minute creatures called by naturalists Noctiluca, animals belonging to the Sub-Kingdom Protozoa. Other animals, such as larval mollusks, Acalephs, and some fishes, contributed toward this light. It was sometimes so intense as to make the light of the stars seem dim in comparison. On the 24th we reached Frontera, and were compelled to wait all day for the little steamer, which brings off passengers and freight from the town. Leaving Frontera we headed toward Veracruz, expecting to reach there on the 25th.

My evenings were all spent on deck enjoying the fresh and invigorating sea air, and in silent contemplation of nature. The phosphorescent water could be plainly seen at the prow of the steamer, and ran away from her bows like molten fire.

CYLINDRELLA.

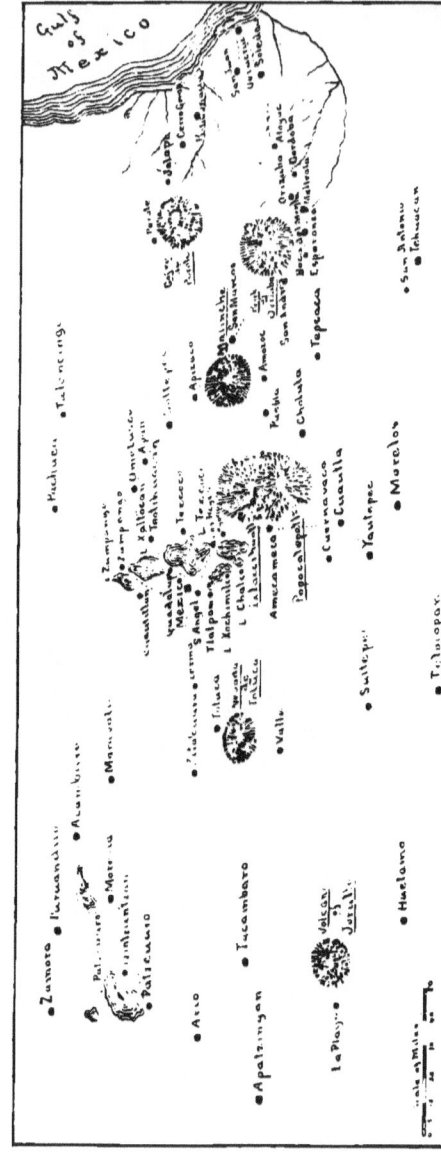

PLATE V.

MAP OF CENTRAL MEXICO.

Note.— The dotted lines thus .... indicate the route of the expedition. Only the principal points are shown, which relate particularly to the work of the party. Words underlined are mountain peaks.

CHAPTER VI.

EARLY on the morning of the 26th we sighted the snow-capped peak of Orizaba, rising above the clouds. It was a grand sight; the sun was shinning brightly, and the clouds about the peak were golden-tinted. It was not a grand sight that met our gaze, as, a few hours later, we sighted the City of Veracruz. A half mile or so of buildings, compact and solid, with blackened domes and steeples; yellow for the most part, scarlet, pink, green, and blue, in patches; a stone landing-quay, and a series of iron cranes projecting from it. To the left was a reddish fort. There were no suburbs, only long, dreary stretches of sand. Very far down on the sand, with the sea breaking over her, was a vessel, wrecked during a recent norther. As we steamed into the harbor, I noted on either side a number of coral reefs which appeared to form atolls. We came to anchor under the lee of the old fort of *San Juan de la Ulua.* The health officers soon appeared, and after their inspection we were permitted to land.

Passengers were obliged, here as in the States, to open their baggage for inspection, and declare any dutiable articles. The Mexican free list included personal clothing, articles worn in use, as watch, cane, etc., and firearms (one or two with their accessories). Each adult male passenger may bring in ninety-nine cigars, forty packages of cigarettes, and one and one-half pounds of snuff or chewing tobacco. Professional men may bring in free the tools pertaining to their professions. The custom house officials we found polite and obliging, and in a very short time we were at liberty to proceed on our journey.

Leaving our baggage at the Hotel Mexico, we called in

a body upon the American Consul.   This gentleman was
very cordial, and gave us much information.   Here we
obtained statistics concerning yellow fever, which were very
interesting,   They showed that for the last three years preceding 1890, there had been but nine deaths from the 'ever.
The following table 1 copied from the official record, and
shows a gradual decrease since 1885.

YELLOW FEVER IN VERACRUZ.

YEAR.	1883	1884	1885	1886	1887	1888	1889	1890
No. of DEATHS.	774	136	328	208	4	3	2	——

The highest month was June, 1883, when 261 deaths
occurred.   The total number of deaths in twenty years was
5493.

From the lighthouse, situated near the quay, we
secured an excellent view of the city and surrounding
country.   Looking seaward, we saw the harbor with its
numerous shipping lying at anchor, the grim old fortress on
the Island of San Juan de la Ulua, the coral reefs stretching
away in the distance, with the waves beating over them,
throwing up a line of white foam.   Inland, the view presented a very interesting scene.   Just back of the city rose
a series of sand dunes, which extended several miles into
the country; and back of these rose a chain of mountains,
looking faint and misty in the distance.   From our high
position the city appeared about a mile square, built upon,
and surrounded by, sand.   The houses were flat roofed and
nearly square, built of stone, and two or three stories in
height.   The only vegetation about the city was low scrubby
bushes and cacti.   The domes were, in some places, black
with buzzards.   In the afternoon we visited the south end
of the town, and walked a little way into the country, but
all we could find were a few dead and bleached shells, and
an occasional lizard of small size.

ATOYAC FALLS

PLATE V.

From Veracruz we sent home our long-neglected let-
ters. The postal regulations of the country are somewhat
peculiar; a letter may be sent to the United States for five
cents, but to any state in Mexico, the charge is fifteen cents.

The following day, at 5:45 A. M., we left Veracruz by the
Mexican Central Railroad for Orizaba. After leaving the
city, the line passed in sight of the Alameda, the cemetery
of Mata, and then crossed the Laguna de Cocos. For the
first few miles we passed over the sandy, chaparral region
which bordered the coast. Near Soledad, twenty-six miles
from Veracruz, we crossed the Rio Jamapa, on a bridge
over four hundred feet long. From this point, the grand
and impressive wonders of the mountains began. From
Soledad to Paso del Macho, we passed through a rocky and
desolate region. Soon the bridge of Alejo was crossed;
this was a handsome structure three hundred and eighteen
feet long, and thirty feet above the stream beneath, which
is a tributary of the Atoyac. Here sugar cane and coffee
plantations began to appear, and the verdure assumed a
more tropical aspect. The trees were covered with those
curious and beautiful parasites, the orchids, and we began
to see what Mexico really was. We now wound around the
base of the Cerro de Chiquihuite, and passed through a tunnel two hundred feet in length. From here we crossed the
Chiquihuite bridge, and soon came in sight of the beautiful
falls of the Atoyac. They certainly presented a most beautiful and picturesque scene, nestled as they were in the
midst of a dense, tropical jungle.

Looking up this ravine we saw the Atoyac river, winding down like a silver thread, and ending in the magnificent
series of falls. Orchids abounded here in great numbers,
and the locality seemed a perfect paradise for a collector.
Mollusks and insects must abound here in great numbers,
and the avifauna must be *par excellence.*

Just before reaching the dépot of Atoyac, we crossed the bridge, three hundred and thirty feet long, spanning the river of the same name. Here the steepest portion of the ascent began, a grade of four per cent., and the double-ender Fairlie locomotive was attached to the train. Between Atoyac and Cordoba, we passed through a fertile country which supported a tropical vegetation. Several small tunnels were passed through, and then we reached Cordoba. At this station a number of natives boarded the train, with fruit to sell, for Cordoba is almost in the center of the tropical fruit region.

From Cordoba the scenery was of surpassing grandeur; the railway slowly wound up the sides of the mountains, while beneath were deep cañons, and the scenery was wild in the extreme. We now passed through five tunnels and crossed three bridges. At the Metlac bridge, crossing the ravine of the same name, we encountered the finest scenery. This bridge was three hundred and fifty feet long, and ninety-two feet above the stream below. The grade here was three per cent. It was a grand, and at the same time a wild sight, to look over the side of that bridge, into the rushing waters below. It was said that in the wet season, the water rose within ten feet of the track. What a grand sight it must be then to make the upward journey. On the bank beside the bridges were little houses, in which lived people who watched for accidents to either bridge or track, and who gave warning to trains if anything was wrong. This was certainly a wise precaution. Soon the valley of Orizaba came in view, and the dépot of that town was soon reached. This is the capital of the State of Veracruz, which state contains over half a million of inhabitants. We were here eighty miles from Veracruz, and one hundred and eighty from the City of Mexico. We were unable to obtain accommodations at the hotel, so were obliged to seek quarters at a *casa de huespedes*, or boarding house. Here we were to spend a week in collecting, and studying the fauna, flora, and Geology.

Orizaba has over twenty thousand inhabitants, and is one of the oldest and quaintest cities in Mexico. The windows of the houses are low and iron grated, as is usual with Spanish towns. Most of the dwellings are but one story in height, built with broad, overhanging eaves, and are composed of morter, sun-dried brick, and a variety of other material. Wood, however, does not enter to any great extent in their construction. The pitched roofs are covered with big red tiles, which serve to throw off the heat of the burning sun, as well as the rain.

There are numerous churches here, several of which are quite imposing structures   Gabriel Barranco, a native artist, has contributed many oil paintings of consider-able merit to many of these churchs.   Earthquakes are frequent here, a fact attested by numerous cracks in the church towers. The steeple of the largest church was thrown down several times by this agency. Several good schools have been established here, and are doing good work. They are supported by the local government. The church party, however, are doing their best to suppress them, but do not seem to succeed. Four schools are for boys, and three for girls.

A river runs through the town, and affords ample power for six or eight mills, which manufacture sugar, cotton, and flour. The surrounding valley is very fertile, and is mostly devoted to the raising of coffee, sugar-cane, and tobacco. The climate is very fine all the year, the average temperature being 75° Fahr. in summer, and very seldom falls below 60° at any time. The valley affords an agreeable medium between the hot lands, and the cold and rarified atmosphere of the Mexico plateau. In this vicinity one sees the orange, lemon, banana, and almond growing at their best, while the coffee, sugar-cane, and tobacco plantations will compare favorably with any in Cuba. Sugar-cane land can be had here for from forty to fifty dollars an acre, which will compare favorably with Louisiana land which sells at one thousand dollars an acre. Cotton is very extensively grown in the State of Veracruz, and thrives up to an elevation of five thousand feet above the sea. According to Mexican statistics, the average product is about two thousand pounds to the acre; this is double the average quantity produced in the United States. The modes of cultivation are very crude, but the wonderful fertility of the soil insures good and remunerative returns, even under these disadvantages. Water is almost the only fertilizer used, and irrigating facilities are excellent.

On the west side of the town is an elevation known as *El Borrego*, or The Goat, where five thousand Mexicans were completely routed by a single company of French Zouaves, during the French invasion. This was a night surprise, wherein the French appeared suddenly among the sleeping Mexicans, and cut them down as fast as they awoke. The importance and superiority of disciplined troops was never more clearly demonstrated than on this occasion. Military discipline is not a characteristic of the Mexican army, as may be seen at any time when they are making a parade. Orizaba, it will be remembered, was for a time the headquarters of General Bazaines' army, and it was here that the French General, finally, in 1866, bade good-by to Maximilian, whose cause he dastardly deserted. Stories are still told here of the outrages committed by the French soldiery.

The streets of the town are in very good condition, paved with lava. The gutters are in the middle of the streets, and the sidewalks are but a few inches in width.

Very few wheeled vehicles are used, the freight being carried almost wholly on the backs of burros and natives. All the produce of the neighboring country, such as vegetables, charcoal, wood, etc., comes in on the backs of natives, men and women, and it is really astonishing to see what heavy loads they will carry for miles over the mountains, at the rate of five or six miles an hour. These natives enjoy wonderful physical health, owing probably to their simple life. They are subject to hardly any deformity, and a hunchbacked native is not to be seen, while it is very rare to meet a maimed or a lame one. Their simple mode of life, living in the open air, and their temperate habits, have earned for them immunity from deformity. What a lesson for our more advanced civilization ! The simple native seldom indulges in pulque, and when he does the effect is far less harmful than our American whisky.

The small plaza is a delightful resort, a perfect wilderness of green with an ornamental fountain in the middle, about which are stone seats. The entire surroundings of Orizaba are garden-like, and the vegetation, owing to the humidity of the atmosphere rising from the Gulf, is always of a vivid green. If we walked through the plaza early in the morning, we would be sure to see many native men and women coming into market from the country, all bending under their weight of provisions, pottery, or some other home product. The women knit as they walk along. Long trains of burros loaded with grain, straw, wood, and alfalfa, are also seen coming in from some hacienda in the valley. The milkmen, too, are seen, with their milk cans, two on each side, suspended from their horses saddles.

It will be remembered that at the little town of Jalapilla, situated a couple of miles from town, Maximilian held the famous council which decided his fate. Had he taken heed to his own common sense, and the advice of his

friends, he would yet be living, and Carlotta would not
have become the insane wreck she was. Veracruz was but
a days' journey away, and a French steamboat lay off San
Juan de la Ulua, ready to convey him across the sea. The
pressure of the church party, his own pride and the con-
fidence of Carlotta, decided his fate.

We employed our few days in Orizaba to good advantage in collecting specimens about the town, and in the
valley, of which there were an abundance. The morning
after our arrival, I took my gun and walked out to see what
sport the valley afforded. The forest bordering the Rio
Blanco, which flowed through the valley, was extremely rich
and picturesque, although the soil was damp. In every
hollow flowed a sparkling brook with crystal waters. The
margins of the river were paradises of leafiness and verdure;
the most striking feature being the variety of ferns, with immense leaves, some terrestrial, others climbing over trees.
I saw here some very large trees; there was one especially,
whose colossal trunk towered up for nearly a hundred feet,
straight as an arrow. Birds along this picturesque river
were very abundant. In several places near the river bank,
the natives had made their little plantations, and built little huts. The people were always cheerful and friendly,
and seemed to be glad to assist us in any manner. King-
fishers, hawks, humming-birds, warblers, and finches, were
seen here in considerable numbers. In the brooks empty-
ing into the Rio Blanco, we found large numbers of
mollusks, the first quantity of living animals of this class
which we had seen while in Mexico.

Physa and *Limnæa* were the most abundant. *L.
cubensis* has a very wide distribution, being found from New
England, where it is known as *L. umbilicata*, west to Missouri,
and south to Cuba and the State of Veracruz. In the woods
bordering the stream we found the Texan Kingfisher, the

Myrtle Warbler, Audubon's Warbler, the common Sparrow Hawk (*Falco sparverius*, a very wide distribution), and several swallows.

The forest was very pleasant for rambling. In some directions broad pathways led down gentle slopes, through almost interminable shrubberies of green foliage, to moist hollows, where the springs of water bubbled up, or shallow brooks ran over their beds of pebbles or muddy floors. The most beautiful road was one that ran through a beautiful grove of lofty trees, crossed the Rio Blanco on a high bridge, and terminated below the high walls of the neighboring hills. Birds and insects were here very plentiful, and many a rare and beautiful specimen was added to our collection. One spot, a few miles from the town, I shall not soon forget; it was on a hill which sloped abruptly towards a boggy meadow, surrounded by woods, through which a narrow winding path continued the slope down to a cool and shady glen, with a brook of cold water flowing at the bottom At mid-day the vertical sun penetrated into the gloomy depths of this romantic spot, lighting up the leafy banks of the stream, where numbers of Scarlet Tanagers and brightly colored butterflies sported about in the stray leaves.

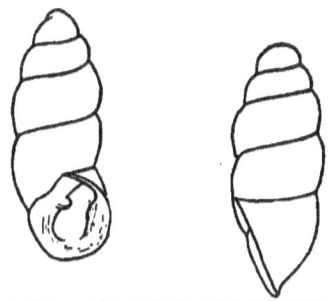

CARYCHIUM MEXICANUM, PILSBRY
(ENLARGED.)

One afternoon we took the street cars for the little village of Nogales, where a large marble quarry was situated. The street car service here was something remarkable. It impressed us the moment we saw it. The cars themselves were quite similar to those used in the States; but the service was certainly unique. The cars were drawn by a couple of burros, which were driven at a run. The

drivers sounded a small horn on approaching the intersection of streets, and everything went with a grand rush.
The mules did not suffer much from this rapid transit pace,
as might be supposed, for they were frequently changed,
and were generally in excellent condition. Our road
ran along the base of the Cerro de Borrego, crossed the
valley of Orizaba, and then again skirted the base of the
hills. Nogales was a neat little village of a few hundred
inhabitants, and was worthy of description. We did not
have time, unfortunately, to form an adequate idea of its
character. The marble yards bordered a deep ravine, through
which flowed a picturesque stream. In the vicinity of the
village we saw several washouts, showing the tremendous
force with which the water must rush down the mountains
during the wet season. On nearly every one of our
excursions, we were greeted by a magnificent view of the
glistening, snow-capped peak of Orizaba, rising high above
the clouds.

One afternoon, a day or two before leaving Orizaba, we
visited a quarry to the east of the town. On our way we
passed through the market place. The scene presented
here was very picturesque and interesting. On the edges
of the sidewalks, and in the streets, were placed little
patches of straw matting, upon which were displayed the
different articles the natives had for sale. Beside the
matting sat native men and women, cross-legged, each one
waiting patiently for some one to come and buy. The
natives were dressed in loose clothes. The men wore white
cotton pants and shirts, and had on their heads straw hats
or *sombreros*. The women wore woolen skirts of a dark
color and cotton waists, over which was thrown a shawl of
a slate color. Everything about them tended to induce
freedom of movement. Their skin was a tawny copper
color, their hair jet black. They appeared inferior in in-

tellect to the Yucatecans, and did not have that quickness of perception noticed in the latter race.

I noted several young girls carrying babies, somewhat after the North American Indian fashion, in their shawls, strung across their backs. They were often seen with the children astraddle their backs. The articles displayed for sale were fruits, sweetmeats, articles of clothing, cutlery, etc. Thursday and Sunday were the principal market days, when the people for miles around flocked in to buy and sell. Milkmen were also seen delivering their mornings milk.

About a mile from the town we reached the quarry. This was not large, and had been worked but a short time. We were fortunate enough to obtain a number of fossils, which gave the geological horizon of the Cretaceous for the region. While several of the party were investigating the quarry, I ascended to the top of the hill, known as the

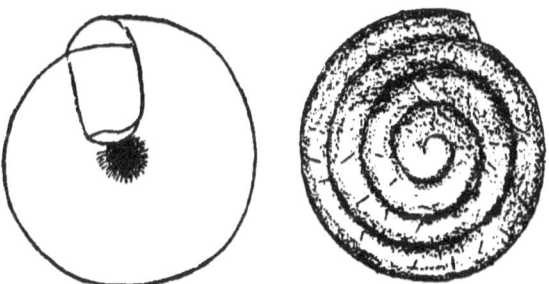

PATULA INTONSA, PILSBRY.

Cerro de Escamela, and had a splendid view of the valley, the best I had as yet enjoyed. This mountain rises 1417 feet above the valley, and has an absolute elevation of 5800 feet.

Crossing this mountain a few hundred feet, I came to a little ravine, where a large number of small mollusks were collected under the wet leaves.   A small *Pupa* (*P. con-tracta*) I found quite abundant.   Among others found were three species of *Patula* (*P. intonsa*, *Pilsbry*), three of *Streptostyla*, and several *Helicina*.   I picked up a *Carychium* (*C. mexicanum*) in great quantities, and a *Proserpina* (*P. Ceres salleana*) of two distinct varieties, one red and one buff.

In the rocks we found the following fossils, all refer-able to the Cretaceous deposits.   *Naricæa castillo*, found imbedded in the marble and identified from a polished sec-tion.   A *Murex* was found, but in such a state as to be un-determinable, so far as specific characters were concerned.   A *Tylostoma* was also found of very large size, but in such a twisted condition as to be unrecognizable.   Several other specimens were found, of which the generic identity could only be determined.   These were *Ostrea*, *Caprina*, and *Hippurites*.

On the second of April we again boarded the Mexico and Veracruz train for another journey skyward, for we had yet some four thousand feet to climb before reaching the Mexi-can plateau.   After leaving Orizaba, the line passed through a fertile valley for a few miles, and then again came to the steep mountain slope.   From Orizaba to Maltrata, the railway ran parallel with the *Rio Blanco*, and crossed its tributaries in several places.   A short time be-fore reaching Maltrata, we passed the *Barranca del In-fiernillo*, or "Ravine of the Little Hell."   This was a wild and desolate place, dropping six hundred feet below the ledge on which the track was laid.   Far below, in the depths of this ravine, was seen a tiny stream, looking like a silver thread, winding its way down.   In this deep gorge the effects of crushing and folding of the rocks was well seen.   The limestone was here standing at every conceiv-able angle, and was overlaid by a huge mass of lava, to

PLATE VII.　　　　　　　　　　　　　　SAN ANDRES.

which the crushing was partly due. Beyond this point we reached the valley of *La Joya*, "The Jewel," in the midst of which lay the town of Maltrata. At Maltrata, all the tropical fruits, such as oranges, limes, citrons, pomegranates, avocato pears, pineapples, bananas, etc., were sold at the lowest prices by girls, who assembled in great numbers when the train arrived. A short stop was made here, and then we proceeded onward and upward.

We now ascended in long, sweeping curves, along a terrace cut in the side of the mountain. In some places, three lines of track could be seen below us, running (apparently) parallel to each other. At *La Bota*, "The Boot," the view was grand. The valley lay stretched out before us, with the little town of Maltrata in the distance, looking like a child's toy. Cows and horses could be made out, and here and there a little lake or stream. The railroad was seen winding its way through like a black thread. Beyond this the mountains rose in the far distance like a blue mist. We soon crossed Winner's bridge, named in honor of the builder, ninety-six feet long and almost as high. It gave one the shivers to look out of the car window, and contemplate as to what would become of us should the train jump the track here, as it often does in the States in such places. I am afraid our friends would never be able to recognize us. From here we passed through a tunnel and came to the *Boca del Monte*, the "Mouth of the Mountain," on the eastern edge of the Mexican plateau. Here the grand scenery ended, and the rest of the ride was through clouds of dust, over a comparatively level country. As we sped along, clouds of dust were continually coming in through the cracks in the windows, making the ride very disagreeable.

At three o clock we reached San Andres Chalchicomula. The depot was situated some four miles off the railroad, and was connected with the town by a tramway. This was

composed of two cars, one for passengers, and one for baggage. We crossed a sandy plain in which grew a few
scrubby bushes; here and there rose huge volcanic cones,
rising to a height of two or three hundred feet. As we entered the town, we noted its similarity to Merida. Here
were the same stone houses and barred windows. We were
now 7973 feet above the sea, and the air was deliciously
cool. We engaged a room at the Hotel de Novedad, and
secured very good accommodations. It had an aspect
which was very pleasing, after our sojourn in the sub-
tropics.

The quaint town of San Andres Chalchicomula contains some four thousand inhabitants, mostly natives. It is
situated at the base of a small plateau, to the southwest of
the Peak of Orizaba; the streets are hilly and narrow, with
wide roads and narrow sidewalks. The principal building
of interest is the Church, situated about the center of the
town. It is built upon a broad terrace, and is quite an imposing structure. Back of the town the hills rise gradually,
finally culminating in the Peak of Orizaba, probably the
highest mountain in North America.

Here I may say that Mexico has three well-defined
climates; hot in the *tierra caliente*, or hot lands of the coast;
temperate in the *tierra templada*, or region lying at an elevation of between three and six thousand feet above the
level of the sea; cold in the *tierra fria*, or regions lying at
an elevation of more than six thousand feet above the level
of the sea. The mean temperatures are as follows:

Tierra caliente 80°.

"   *templada 70°.*

"   *fria 60°.*

CHAPTER VII.

We found both the fauna and flora of San Andres to differ greatly from that of Orizaba, four thousand feet below. Here were pine and spruce scattered about, and other trees of the temperate climate. The birds were quite perceptably different; here jays, resembling our Florida Blue Jay,  Chewinks, Purple Finches, sparrows, Golden-winged Woodpeckers, Cross-bills, and snow-birds, were seen. We seemed to have stepped from the tropics into the temperate region. The Broad-tailed Humming-bird was tolerably common. Every day, in the cooler hours of the morning or even-

MEXICAN CROSSBILL.

ing, they were seen whirling about the bushes. Their habits are unlike those of all other birds. They dart to and fro so swiftly that the eye can scarcely follow them, and when they stop before a flower it is only for a few moments. They poise themselves in an unsteady manner, their wings moving rapidly; probe the flower, and then shoot off for another part of the shrub. Sometimes two males close with each other and fight, mounting upward in the struggle, and then hastily separating and darting back to their work. Their brilliant colors cannot be seen while they are flutter-ing about, and the different species are difficult to distin-guish. This species was the only one seen, although I believe others are to be found in the region.

We were somewhat astonished at the utter absence of insect life, which was quite a contrast from Orizaba, where we had seen them in great numbers. The country between San Andres and the Peak of Orizaba was cut up into deep gullies or barrancas, in which we found several species of birds. The soil here was volcanic, consisting of ash, cinders, and lava, which had flowed from Orizaba. From the bluff, back of the town, we enjoyed many a fine view of the surrounding country, showing us a flat plain, covered with large and small volcanic cones. Every morning we were greeted by a fine view of the white peak.

Near San Francisco, a small village some two miles from San Andres, the Maguey plant was cultivated to a great extent. This is the plant from which the famous Mexican drink, *pulque*, is made. It is gathered in the following manner: when the central shoot, which produces the flower, appears, they cut out the whole heart, leaving nothing but the thick walls, which makes a natural basin, two feet in depth and one and one-half in diameter. Into this opening the sap flows, and is removed twice or three times daily. It is collected in a large gourd, called an *acojate*, having a horn at one end and a square hole at the other, through which the sap is drawn by suction. This sap, before fermentation, is called *aguamil* or honey water. It is carried into the towns in sheep-skin barrels, with the hair inside. The Mexicans derive an immense revenue from this plant, many plantations yielding ten or twelve thousand dollars annually.

This being Holy Week, we were not able to make arrangements for the ascent of Orizaba until the close of the festivities. On Holy Thursday, in the evening, we walked about the town, having a good opportunity to observe the customs of the people on festival days. The streets were crowded with people walking up and down. On the corners of the streets, and especially in the plaza, were men with tables before them, upon which were placed for sale ice-cream, sweet-cakes, and various kinds of confectionary. In some places small trinkets and other articles of merchandise replaced the ice-cream. The municipal building was lighted with candles, and presented a very pretty appearance. The church was decorated very tastefully, and was lighted by a multitude of candles; some were strung about the sides of the church, while others hung in long pendents from the roof. The altars were all covered up, and had but few candles before them. The whole effect was at once pretty and impressive.

People were passing to and fro from the church in a continuous stream. Wishing to see more of the church, we edged our way through the crowd and entered. Before the covered altars were kneeling people in every station of life. The proprietors of haciendas and the poor natives were side by side; richly dressed ladies and native girls in rags were kneeling together, their dresses touching. In fact, the solemnity of the occasion seemed to bring all classes to the same level. Throughout the whole church not a sound was heard. The people stepped softly, and spoke not a single word inside the church during the time we were in it. We were afterwards told that it was the custom to perform their devotions on this day in silence.

On the 6th of April, we set out for the ascent of Orizaba (called by the Aztecs, *Citlaltepetl*, or Mountain of the Star) with eleven guides and carriers, and several burros. Besides our guns, ammunition, and other collecting utensils, we had provisions for three days, consisting of eggs, bread, oranges, dried beef, and a cask of water. Our road led over a sandy plain, slightly ascending. After following this for four or five miles, we reached the forests of pine and spruce. At this point the ascent became very steep, and the burros labored very heavily under their burdens. Here the song of the robin was heard, and blue-jays were seen in abundance. We might easily have imagined ourselves in a New England pine forest. The trees here were noble ex-

amples of arboreal growth, many of them being over a
hundred feet high, and running up as straight as an arrow.
The ground was covered with pine kneedles, making a floor
as soft as velvet, and the odor was delicious.

At a height of 10,750 feet, we halted for lunch, and to
give the burros a rest. The thermometer here registered
63° Fahr., and the air was quite chilly. We must have presented a rather wild appearance, dressed as we were in all
manner of costumes, with the natives in their white pants
and jackets and wide brimmed sombreros, with revolvers
sticking from their belts! After a half hours rest we again
proceeded up the mountain. Now and then we caught
glimpses of the world below, with its valleys, towns, and
clouds. The up-grade soon became terrific, and the burros
could hardly carry us along. Evidences of volcanic action
now appeared on every hand, in the shape of huge blocks
of lava, and cinders. Here the vegetation began to thin
out, the pines disappearing, but the spruces still keeping
on, though the trees were smaller and less numerous than
lower down. The Sierra Negra was seen on our right, and
through a cleft in the mountains we caught occasional
glimpses of the peak. Another level plain was crossed, a
stony path ascended, and then a full and magnificent view
of the peak burst upon our sight.

We made our camp, for the night, on a ledge jutting
from the side of the mountain. Here we prepared our supper, and endeavored to spend a comfortable night. As the
sun set the cold became intense, and our thick blankets
were scarcely adequate to keep us from suffering severely
from the low temperature. Nothing occurred to disturb
our rest, save the howling of coyotes and the uneasiness of
the burros in their cramped quarters. Our camp was at an
altitude of over 13,000 feet, and as yet none of us experienced any difficulty from the rarified atmosphere.

OUR CAMP ON ORIZABA.—13,000 FEET ALT

PLATE VIII.

Next morning (April 7th), at four o'clock, we turned
out, ate a light meal, and started for the peak on foot. We
were well protected from the cold by extra jackets, which
we had brought with us. To prevent us from slipping on
the ice, we wore stockings over our shoes. Leaving the
ledge of rock where we had spent the night, we first passed
over a comparatively level plain, covered with tufts of dried,
half-dead grass. The soil here was sandy, and progression
difficult. A gentle incline was soon reached, which carried
us to the foot of the peak proper. Here the last vestige of
vegetation disappeared, and we were surrounded by black
and barren blocks of lava. Soon the rise was at an angle
of thirty-five degrees, and the climbing became very fatiguing. One of our party soon showed signs of giving out,
and complained of pains in his head and stomach; he also
had a desire to lie down and go to sleep. At a height of
14,000 feet, he was obliged to succumb and return to the
camp. Now the ascent was over huge boulders and
crumbling stones, and in many places a few steps forward
were followed by one backwards. From our present elevation we were enabled to view the country for many miles.
Way off in the distance were seen the snow-capped peaks of
Popocatepetl and Ixtaccihuatl, sister peaks to Orizaba.
Down in the valley below was seen the town of San Andres,
appearing like a child's toy, and scattered over the plain
were towns and villages in every direction.

Frequent rests were now taken, for the rarified air was
beginning to tell on the rest of us. At one of our resting-
places, I had the good fortune to observe the clouds rising
slowly from the valley. As they rose higher and higher,
peak after peak was covered, until a level sea of clouds lay
before me, with here and there a point appearing above it
like an island in the midst of a sea. It was the most beautiful sight I had ever seen. Again we arose and stumbled

on. The guides were now some distance ahead, and we followed on as quickly as possible. Soon the snow-field was reached, and here the truly difficult part of the ascent began. The field was cut up into little hillocks, which rendered progression over it much easier than it would have been, had it been a smooth field of frozen snow. When within three hundred feet of the summit, I was seized with the most violent symptoms. My head swam, my eyes be· came bloodshot, and my stomach felt very qualmish. A ringing noise entered my ears, and I was obliged to desist from ascending further. Another of my companions was affected in the same manner, and but one was able to reach the actual summit, and he had to be hauled up with ropes by the natives. Our descent was somewhat novel. A native had carried with him a piece of straw matting, and upon this we sat and were pulled down a sandy incline of thirty-five degrees, in much the same manner that coasting is done in Canada. We arrived at the camp foot-sore and weary, and were glad enough to lie down and rest.

Our determination showed that the height formerly given for the mountain is too low. After making allowances for slight variations, the height of the mountain is 18,200 feet. The barometer, at the summit, read 15.56 inches, and the temperature was 35° Fahr. During the ascent of the second day, the barometer indicated a drop of .1 inch. In 1796, Ferrer, by means of angle measurements taken from the Encero, determined the height to be 17,879 feet. Humboldt, a few years later, measured the mountain from a plain, near the town of Jalapa, and obtained 17,375 feet. He observed, however, that his angles of elevation were very small, and the base-line difficult to level. In 1877, a Mexican scientific commission, composed of MM. Plowes, Rodriguez, and Vigil, made the ascent of the volcano from the side of San Andres, and determined the

PEAK OF ORIZABA

height to be 17,664 feet. Dr. Kaska, not long since, determined, by a mercurial thermometer, the height to be
18,045 feet. Should our deductions prove correct, then
Orizaba, and not Popocatepetl, must take the first place
among the mountains of North America. The second night
was passed like the first, in hugging the fire. Early on the
following morning we returned to San Andres, reaching
there late in the afternoon. The only life observed on the
peak was a Sparrow Hawk, a raven, and a few small lizards.

Before leaving San Andres, a word concerning its avi-.
fauna may not be out of place. As before said, the difference between the birds of San Andres and those of Orizaba,
4,000 feet below, was marked. Only three species were
common to both localities. Nearly all species belonged to
northern genera. In the town, the only birds observed
were the House Finch, Blue Grosbeak, and Barn Swallow.
In the sandy stretch of country, between San Andres and
the pine woods, on the slopes of Orizaba, the most characteristic species were sparrows, thrushes, the Black-eared
Bush Tit, Brown and Mexican Towhee. In the pine forest
the American Robin, Bluebird, Mexican Chickadee, Sumichrast's Jay, and Audubon's Warbler, were abundant. A
peculiar fact observed was that none of the characteristic
birds of the open country were found on the wooded part
of the mountain. Snowbirds and Sumichrast's Jay, however, were found on the plain some distance from the edge
of the forest. Of the other branches—mollusks, insects,
etc.—we saw nothing, save a few lizards. The following
day we left San Andres for the City of Mexico, arriving at
the latter place at midnight. We put up at the Hotel
Humboldt, situated on the Calle de Jesus, where we
secured very excellent accommodations.

CHAPTER VIII.

WHAT Paris is to France, the City of Mexico is to the Mexican Republic. The city derived its name from the Aztec war-god Mexitli. It is a large metropolis, containing something over three hundred thousand inhabitants, embracing a large diversity of nationalities. When Cortez first saw the city, in 1519, it was said to measure nine miles in circumference, and to contain half a million inhabitants. This statement is probably greatly exaggerated. The ancient Aztec Capital, bearing the name of Tenochtitlan, was completely destroyed by Cortez, who established on its site the present city. The streets of the city are broad and straight, lined with two-story houses, and there are also several spacious avenues and boulevards. The houses are built mostly of stone, covered with stucco; the windows opening upon little balconies, shaded by awnings of different colors. They are built after the usual Spanish style, with a central courtyard. The open areas about which the houses are built often present most pleasing displays of fountains, flowers, and statuary. On the main street, leading from the plaza to the alameda, are several private residences, having very handsome courts, or *patios*, as they are called, filled with the most beautiful flowers, and rendered musical by the singing of caged birds.

Upon these areas, which are open to the sky, the inner doors and windows open, the second story being furnished with a walk and balustrade running round the patio. Heavy doors, studded with nails, shut off this patio from the street at night.

The houses of the capital are substantially built, the walls being of great thickness, and composed of stuccoed bricks. The roofs are nearly all flat and without chimneys; there is no provision made for artificial heat, nor indeed is there need of any in a climate where the temperature seldom falls below 60° Fahr. It is always warm in the middle of the day, and cool in the morning and evening. The climate is temperate, and the atmosphere very dry. Fires, on account of the indestructibility of the houses, are a rare occurrence.

The main thoroughfares enter and depart from the *Plaza Major*. Some are broad and some narrow, but all are paved, straight, and clean. The street car service is excellent. All the cars depart from the main plaza in front of the cathedral. They are always in a hurry; the mules are driven very rapidly through the crowded thoroughfares, yet no accidents happen. Funerals are conducted by turning one of these cars into a hearse, or catafalque, another car being reserved for the mourners and pall-bearers. A long string of these cars may sometimes be seen gliding into the suburbs, where the grave-yards are located. The drivers of the cars blow cow-horns at the intersection of the streets, to warn people off the track. The fact that all the cars leave and enter the Plaza Major, makes it comparatively easy for a stranger to find his way around the city and surrounding suburbs. The central plaza of every Mexican city and town, is always the central park.

The streets of Mexico intersect each other at right angles, and are so nearly alike that it is a little puzzling for the stranger to find his way about them. Another drawback is the awkward manner of naming the streets, each block of a single street having a different name. This subdivision is, however, to be entirely discarded, and in a few years the streets will be named like those of our northern cities. The Paseo de la Reforma is the principal boulevard, and connects the city with Chapultepec. It is over two miles in length and over one hundred feet in width; it has double avenues of Eucalyptus shade trees on either side, with stone sidewalks and seats, placed at short intervals, made of the same material. At certain places the paseo widens into a *glorieta*, or circle, four hundred feet in diameter, in which are placed handsome statues. The first contains the statue of Columbus, by Cordier, a very handsome and artistic piece of work. Another circle contains the equestrian statue of Charles IV, of colossal size, thirty tons of metal being used in the casting. It is said to be the largest casting ever made. Another *glorieta* contains the statue of the native martyr Guatemozin, the last of the Aztec emperors. There are in all six of these circles, all of which are destined to contain a fine monument. Maximilian named this drive the Boulevarde Emperiale; but on the restoration of the Rebuplic the name was changed to the one by which it is now called. In the afternoon the paseo is thronged with a motley crowd of people driving, riding on horseback, or promenading; dashing equestrians in gay attire; tally-ho coaches conveying merry parties of tourists; and here and there a mounted policeman in fancy uniform. Among the pedestrians are well-dressed gentlemen in broadcloth suits, mingled with whom are the common class of people in their picturesque costumes. The women lend color to the scene by their red and blue rebosas, drawn tightly over the shoulders, or tied across the chest, securing an infant to the back. Nothing more picturesque can be imagined than this ever changing crowd. Carriages go out towards Chapultepec on one side of the paseo and return on the other, leaving the central portion of the roadway exclusively for equestrians. Another boulevard, known as the Paseo de la Viga, runs along the banks of the Xochimilco canal, but since the completion of the new paseo, this has ceased to be the favorite resort for driving.

The horses seen on the paseo, as well as all of the horses in Mexico, are of Arabian descent and are splendid animals. They are medium-sized, high-spirited, with small ears, and a broad chest expanded by the rarified air of the high altitude. The saddles and trappings are gorgeous with silver ornaments, without any regard for tastefulness whatever; eighteen or twenty inches of leather, fancifully worked, are often attached to each stirrup. The Mexican rider wears a short leather jacket, set off by a dozen or more silver buttons, tight leather pantaloons, heavy with silver buttons, partially opened at the side and flaring at the bottom. Instead of a vest, he wears a frilled linen shirt. This is set off by a scarlet scarf, tied about the waist. His spurs are of silver and frequently weigh half a pound each, while the rowels are an inch long. These spurs are more for show than use, however. On his head he wears a huge sombrero of brown felt, the brim being ten or twelve inches broad, and the crown measuring the same in height. In addition there is a silver or gold cord placed about the crown, and frequently the wearer's monogram is worked in silver on the side.

The soldiers quartered in the government building were frequently seen parading in the plaza. The Mexican soldier has neither shoes nor stockings, shoes being replaced by sandals. The discipline is of the crudest sort; when marching they do not keep step, but move at will; it is a curious sight to see a company marching, with a band at their head, all keeping out of step, even the band. One would suppose the band, at least, would keep step, but such is not the case, although they are fine musicians. The troops wear linen or cotton uniforms, with silver buttons. On dress parades they wear a plain uniform of dark blue.

One of the most interesting objects in Mexico is the famous Cathedral, fronting upon the Plaza Major. Ninety

years of labor, and several millions of dollars, were spent
in its construction.   The edifice stands on the spot which
was once occupied by the great Aztec Teocalli, or temple,
dedicated to the war-god of the nation.   The Spaniards
destroyed the ancient temple, as soon as they became
masters of the country, and built a church upon its site;
this was soon after pulled down, and the present edifice
erected in its place.   The ancient temple was said to have
been pyramidal in form, the summit one hundred and fifty
feet above the ground, reached by broad stone steps.   Human sacrifices were said to have been made here daily; wars
were made with neighboring tribes to supply victims for the
altar.   The accounts of the Spanish chroniclers are probably
greatly exaggerated, if not pure fabrications.   The façade
of the present edifice, at each side of which rises a massive
tower, crowned by a bell-shaped dome, is divided by but-
tresses into three parts.   The towers are each over two
hundred feet in height, of Doric and Ionic architecture.   In
the western tower is the great bell, named after the patron
saint of Mexico, Santa María de Guadalupe, which measures
nineteen feet in height, being the largest, in size and
weight, in the world.   The basso-relievos, statues, and
friezes of the façade are of white marble.   The structure
measures over four hundred feet in length, and two hundred
in width, and is in shape like a cross.   Its roof is supported
by pillars, each thirty-five feet in circumference, and is one
hundred and seventy-five feet from the floor.   The high
altar was once the richest in the world, but during the various revolutions, this—and the other six—has been de-
spoiled, and millions of dollars have been put in circulation
from it.   The candlesticks were of solid gold, and the
statue of the Assumption was of the same metal, and studded
with rubies and diamonds.   But with all its losses, the
church is decorated as no other on the American Continent.

THE CATHEDRAL

PLATE X

The railing of the choir gallery was manufactured in China, and was said to have cost one and a half millions of dollars. An offer to replace it in solid silver was refused. On the sides of the church there are over a dozen chapels, inclosed in bronze gates, in one of which the body of Iturbide, the first Mexican Emperor, is buried. Two valuable paintings hang upon the walls, one a Murillo, and the other an original Michael Angelo. The dim light which pervades the interior of the Cathedral, tempered by the light of the tall candles, lends a weirdness to the scene, but the effect, generally, is not so good as that rendered by our stained windows. Here, in 1864, Maximilian and Carlotta were crowned Emperor and Empress of Mexico.

The view from the top of the Cathedral is grand, and should be seen by every tourist. It was from a height like this that Cortez first beheld the beauties of the valley of Anahuac. At our feet lies the plaza, with its tree-dotted Zocalo, while the entire city is spread out before us. Not far away looms against the sky the tall castle of Chapultepec, while the towers of Guadalupe come still nearer the vision. The distant fields of Maguey, the smooth waters of the lakes, and the tall, sky-reaching elevations of Popocatepetl and Ixtaccihuatl, make a scene which it is no wonder Humboldt declared to be the most beautiful eye ever rested on. We can almost see the elevated path between the two mountains over which Cortez, in 1520, and Scott, in 1847, led their conquering hosts. The front of the Cathedral is always beseiged by beggars and lottery venders. Sometimes the lottery vender is a man who importunes you to purchase; sometimes a young girl, and at others, even a child of ten or twelve years. The Mexican Government realizes fully a million dollars per annum from licenses granted to protect this business; rich and poor alike invest, the difference being only in the amount; strangers smother their scruples and purchase tickets, thus adding their mite to the iniquitous business.

The City of Mexico is famous for its large number of scientific, literary, and charitable institutions, its many primary and advanced schools, and its well-appointed hospitals. The national palace covers the whole eastern side of the Plaza Major, and has a frontage of nearly or quite seven hundred feet; it occupies the site of the ancient palace of Montezuma. The present building was erected in 1693. The palace is two stories in height, and has a tower over the central doorway. It contains the suite of rooms belonging to the President, and those belonging to the various departments of state. The Hall of Ambassadors is interesting on account of the collection of life-size portraits of Mexican rulers, most of whom were either exiled or executed as traitors. Here also is a good portrait of Washington, and a battle-piece, by a native artist, representing the battle of Puebla, where the French were so completely defeated. An apartment known as Maximilian's room is shown to the visitor, situated in the corner of the palace, having two windows, one overlooking the plaza, and the other the public market. The Hall of Iturbide, hung in rich crimson damask, displaying the eagle and serpent, the arms of Mexico, is also shown. In the rear of the palace are the General Post-office and the National Museum. In the patio of the palace a small botanical garden is maintained, which contains many domestic and exotic trees and plants, several of which are very rare and curious. The rare and extraordinary plant, *Cheirostemon platanifolium*, is shown in the garden. This remarkable curiosity is called the hand-tree, and is covered with bright scarlet flowers, almost exactly in the shape of the human hand. But three specimens of this plant are known to exist in Mexico.

In the rear of the national palace is the Academy of

Fine Arts—known as the Academy of San Carlos,—which contains many fine paintings by Vinci, Valasquez, Titian, Rubens, Perugino, and others. The paintings are situated on the second floor, while on the first floor there is a large hall of sculpture, containing casts of many classic statues. The art gallery is full of interest; it contains several priceless paintings by the old masters, as well as a large number of admirable pictures by native talent, which are remarkable for their execution. Two large canvases by Jose Maria Velasco, representing the Valley of Mexico, form fine and striking landscapes, which are surpassed by but few modern painters. The gem of the Academy, however, is, without doubt, the large painting by Felix Parra, a native artist, entitled "Las Casas protecting the Aztecs from slaughter by the Spaniards." This artist has given us an original conception most perfectly carried out. He is but thirty years of age, and has already made himself famous. The painting received first prize at the Academy of Rome. The Academy also contains an art school free to the youth of the city, and is assisted by the government to the amount of $35,000 annually. Prizes are given for meritorious work; one annual prize is especially sought for, namely, an allowance of $600 a year for six years, to enable the recipient to study art abroad. The school is free to all, and the son of the peon has as good a right as he with the wealthiest parents. The institution is in a flourishing condition, but lacks the stimulus of an appreciative community to encourage its growth, and much emulation among its pupils.

The native has always been a lover of the artistic and beautiful. The Aztec pictures were but early examples of this love struggling to assert itself. There are numerous paintings preserved in the National Museum, which are beautiful specimens of art. Some of these are on deerskin, and some on papyrus made from the leaves of the

Maguey plant. The art of metal casting and the manufacture of cotton cloth was known to the ancient Toltecs and Aztecs. There are numerous examples still preserved, which show that the Aztec was an admirable worker in silver and gold. Cortez, in his hurry to send gold back to his sovereign, caused everything made of this precious metal to be consigned to the melting pot, and thus many fine specimens of the work were destroyed. Were specimens of these golden and silver ornaments now existing, they would be worth many times their weight in gold. The art, however, has been handed down from one generation to another, and the modern native can produce silver filigree work superior to anything made elsewhere. The native women also make the most exquisite pictures from colored pieces of straw, representing scenery and buildings with wonderful accuracy. They also make wax figures representing scenes and types of Mexican life. On San Francisco street, these statuettes may be seen reproducing the different types of Mexican life with wonderful fidelity. Another branch of art, which the ancient, as well as the modern Aztec excells in, is the production of feather work. The gorgeous plumage of parrots, humming-birds, trogans, and orioles, are especially adapted for this work. In ancient times the feathers were glued upon cotton-web, and made into dresses to be worn on festal occasions. There is preserved, in the museum, a beautiful robe of this character said to have been worn by Montezuma II. This industry has been inherited by the modern Aztecs, and pictures and small landscapes may be purchased anywhere in the city for a moderate sum.

Not far from the Academy of Fine Arts is the National Conservatory of Music, founded in 1553. Near at hand, also, is the National Library, where there is a collection of nearly two hundred thousand volumes, many of them being of extreme rarity. Here are to be found volumes of price-less value, among which is a large volume of painted pictures, said to be original dispatches from Montezuma to his allies, and captured by Cortez. The library contains books in all languages, dating from the present century, back four hundred years or more. It has no systematic arrangement or catalogue. The library building is an old convert which was confisicated for the purpose The iron fence, which encloses the edifice, is ornamented by marble busts of famous scientists, authors, and orators, and the plat of ground in front is graced by a beautiful bed of flowers.

The Plaza Major, as before said, is the center of the city in every sense of the word. It is fully one thousand feet square and is beautifully laid out. In the center is the Zocalo, screened with groups of orange-trees, shrubbery, and flowers. Here, in a circular music stand, the military band gives concerts four times weekly, in the afternoon and evening. At the western side of the Zocalo is the flower market, whose perfume fills the atmosphere and whose beauty delights the eye. The market is presided over by pretty native girls, who importune you to buy the choice nosegays, and seldom is their entreaty in vain. The ancient Aztec was an intense lover of flowers; he used them in all his ceremonies, even to those of the sacrifice; the modern native has lost none of his affection for these beautiful emblems, and uses them on every occasion. The most abundant flowers seen here are red and white roses, pinks of various colors, heliotrope, violets, poppies, both white and scarlet, and forget-me-nots. These flowers are artistically arranged in large bouquets, with a backing of maiden-hair ferns, and are sold for fifteen cents each. The price, however, is not fixed, and one may easily purchase a bouquet for half the sum first named.

The principal market-place is situated near the plaza, at its southwest end, a block away. Sunday morning is the great market day of the week, the same as in all Mexican cities. Each line of trade has its special location, and the confusion of tongues, while bartering is going on, would silence the New York Stock Exchange. Occasionally, in the market, one will witness the Mexican style of saluting each other. This they do by embracing, and patting each other on the back in a most demonstrative manner. This seems rather a queer salutation for individuals of the same sex.

A tourist soon becomes acquainted with the topography of the city. The chief business street leads from the railroad dépot to the Plaza Major. The most fashionable street for shopping is that known as the Street of the Silversmiths. This is nearly a mile in length, and of good width. The streets are mostly named from churches or convents standing on or near them. One street is named the Street of the Holy Ghost, after the church of the same name, situated near by. The Calle de San Francisco is another of the business thoroughfares devoted to businesses of all kinds. The streets near the Plaza Major, and Alameda, are lighted by electricity, other portions of the city proper by gas, and the outlying districts by oil-fed lanterns. One object, always observable in the city at night, is the lantern of the policeman placed in the middle of the junction of the streets, with the policeman himself standing beside it. The police system of the city is excellent, and very few street brawls happened during our six weeks' sojourn.

The shops of Mexico, instead of having the name of the proprietor over the entrance, as in the United States, are all named; some of these names are worthy of record, and

I give below a list of some of the most important, which were situated near our hotel:

La Ciudad de Mexico.	The City of Mexico.
Abarrotes por Mayor y Menor.	Bargains for better or worse.
Al Progreso.	To Progress.
Làs Fabricas de Francia.	The Manufactures of France.
El Tigre.	The Tiger.
Providencia.	Providence.
Los Dos Amicos.	The Two Friends.
La Diadema.	The Diadem.
El Nacional.	The National.
Botica de Porta Galli.	Drug store of the Gate of Heaven.

This last is very appropriate, for the contents of a drug store.

The hotels of Mexico will not compare favorably with those of the States. The Iturbide is the largest and most fashionable in the city, and is patronized by nearly all tourists. It is a spacious building, situated near the Plaza Major, and once served as the palace of Augustin de Iturbide, the first Emperor of Mexico. All the chambermaids in the hotels here are men, and very good servants they make. In the selection of a sleeping apartment the tourist should select one facing the east or south, thus securing an abundance of sunshine.

Regarding places of amusement, the city contains several theatres, and a circus. The best and most fashionable theatre is the Teatro Nacional, built in 1844, having a seating capacity of three thousand persons. Here are held the commencement exercises of the military school of Chapultepec. A good opera company is engaged for a short annual season, but French, Spanish, and Italian Opera can be seen here the year round. Three other theatres, the Arbeu, the Hidalgo, and the Coliseo Viejo, are very good; there are also several others, open Sundays, but those are

rather to be avoided than sought after.   There is a spacious
bull-ring at the northern end of the paseo, where exhibitions
are given to crowded houses on Sundays and festal days.
The sport, however, is cruel and barbaric, and, although
we patronized it on one occasion, yet the tourist had better
forego this brutal entertainment.   At the bull-fight which
we attended, several horses were butchered, four or
five bulls killed, and several men nearly lost their lives.

One of the most admirable establishments in the city
is the Monte de Piedad (signifying "The Mountain of
Mercy").   It was founded by Count Regla, the owner of
the Real del Monte silver mine, more than a century ago,
who gave the sum of $300,000 for the purpose, in order
that the poor might obtain advances on personal property
at a low and reasonable rate of interest.   Any article deposited for this purpose is valued by two disinterested persons, and three-fourths of its value is advanced. If the owner
ceases to pay the interest on the loan the article is kept
six months longer, when it is exposed for sale at a marked
price.   After six months more have passed, if the article is
not disposed of, it is sold at public auction, and all that
is realized above the sum which was advanced, together
with the interest, is placed to the credit of the original
owner.   This sum, if not called for in a given time, reverts
to the bank.   The establishment has also a safety vault,
where all sorts of valuables are stored for safe keeping.
One dollar is the smallest amount loaned, and ten thousand
is the largest.

The Museo Nacional, situated in the rear of the national
palace, is of surpassing interest to the naturalist and anti-
quarian, and we visited it soon after our arrival.   As we
entered, after ascending two flights of stairs, the first thing
we saw was a gigantic cast of the *Megatherium Cuvieri*.   In
this room were also a few minerals.   To the left of this

room we entered the Department of Palæontology. Here were displayed a number of very well preserved fossils, but, curiously enough, there were none from Mexico, all of them being from European and North American beds. At the farther end of the room were a number of plaster casts of extinct animals, mostly Plesiosauri and other saurians of the Jurassic and Liassic periods. To the right of the entrance was the Mineralogical Department. Here, for the first time we saw specimens from Mexico. The marbles, agates, precious metals, calcites, etc., were well represented. The arrangement was according to Dana, and the labels, all handsomely printed with the scientific and common names, locality, and formula, numbered according to his system. Larger labels were attached to the backs of the cases, and designated to what group the specimens belonged. In the center of the hall was a gigantic stalactite, four feet in length, from the "*Gruta de Cacahuamilpa.*"

In the next hall beyond, we came to the Department of Mammalogy. The collection was fairly well represented by a number of carefully mounted specimens. Here we saw a very good specimen of the rare *Hyrax capensis*, enclosed in a handsome glass case. This animal, from Australia, is exceedingly rare, but few museums possessing specimens of it, and the Museo Nacional is to be congratulated in possessing so fine and rare a specimen.

To the right was a case of Anthropoid apes; beyond this a case containing representatives of the Family Felidæ. Here were several fine specimens of *Felis pardalis*, *Felis onca*, and *Felis concolor*, all from Mexico. We next came to a case containing a fine collection of the Skunks. Among these a good series of the *Mephites mephitica* and *Mephites macrura*. Other specimens of note in this case were *Lutra fulma* and *Galictis vittata*. In the next case were representatives of the domestic cat, *Felis domestica*, and in the center of the hall a good sized horizontal case in which a number of foreign and native animals were displayed. At the end of the hall was a finely mounted specimen of the Asiatic Elephant, *Elephas indicus*. In the flat cases over the central ones were arranged a number of insects, quite well preserved, but poorly named. '

The next hall was devoted to the Department of Ornithology, and here we found the richest collection of the museum. Arranged in wall cases about the hall were several hundred birds, native and exotic. Among the native birds were Andubon's Warbler, Sumichrast's Jay, Mexican Tohee, and a number of the birds obtained by us at Orizaba and San Andres. Among the exotic birds were the rare New Zealand Parrot, *Strigops habroptilus*, and the beautiful Bird of Paradise, *Paradisia reggiana*. Also the Golden Turkey, *Meleagris ocellata*. Nearly all the larger orders were represented, forming, upon the whole, a very good generic collection. A few eggs and nests were tastefully arranged in the lower compartments of several cases. Most of the birds were correctly named. In this hall were also several mammals and a few cases of insects.

The next hall was devoted to Anthropology. Here was a case of skulls (casts), showing the form of the head of different races; a case containing pieces of tanned human skin, and several alcoholic specimens of human fœta; two cases of human skulls with a few photos, showing types of Mexican natives; a skull in a case showing different parts, a very good skeleton, and two mummies.

In the next hall, beyond, was exhibited a fairly good collection of reptiles, fishes, etc. This collection was represented by a number of alcoholic and stuffed specimens. Here I saw better stuffed fishes than are to be seen in many of our museums in the United States.

The alcoholic collection was very neatly and tastefully

HALL OF ANTIQUITIES.

PLATE XI

arranged. In the central cases were a number of exotic shells, mostly wrongly named. The hall devoted to the Mollusca and lower invertebrates was in the worst condition of all, as regards naming. In the Mollusca such errors as the following were common:

Cyp. talpa	*for*	*C. exanthema.*	
Murex erinaceus	"	*M. salleanus.*	
" *inflatus*	"	*M. ramosus.*	
" *haustellum*	"	*M. brandaris.*	
" *triqueter*	"	*M. erinaceus.*	

The most ludicrous error was the following, in which *Murex brassica* was named for a bivalve, *Pinna squamosa.* The shells were wholly without systematic arrangement, bivalves and univalves being mixed in hopeless confusion. The remainder of the collection consisted of mounted crustaceans, sea-urchins, star-fishes, corals, and alcoholic specimens of the lower types. In one of the cases was a very good collection of glass models, by Blaschka, of sea-cucumbers, sea-anemones, and other invertebrates. Upon the whole, the museum was very tastefully arranged, and reflected great credit upon its curator.

On the ground floor was the hall of antiquities, and here reposed the remains of the ancient Aztec temples and their gods. Among the most interesting antiquities were the sacrificial stone, the Palenque cross, and the calendar stone. This calendar stone was an exceeding curious and remarkable example of Aztec sculpture. It represented the principal division of the Aztec year into days, months, etc. It has been written upon more extensively than any other single example of ancient workmanship. It was for a time imbedded in the western tower of the cathedral, but was removed a short time ago and now rests in its appropriate place in the National Museum. Among the other noted sculptures were Huitzilopochtli, the Aztec god of war; Quetzalcoatl, the coiled serpent, and Chaacmol, the tigerking, discovered by Dr. Le Plongeon, in Yucatan, some years ago. At the organization of the national government, in 1867, a sum of five hundred dollars per month was voted for the expenses of this institution. It publishes a bulletin called the Anales del Museo Nacional de Mexico, the first number of which appeared in 1877, containing articles by Señores Mendoza, Sanchez, Orozco y Berra, and Bárcena. They have appeared with regularity, and constitute a most valuable addition to the literature of Anahuac.

CHAPTER IX,

One of the pleasantest excursions in the environs of the capital is to the Castle of Chapultepec, or "Hill of the Grasshopper." It is situated at the end of the Paseo de la Reforma. About Chapultepec are gathered more of the grand memories of this interesting country than any other spot in America. Here the Aztec kings deposited their treasures and made their homes. Here, also, the ill-fated Maximillian established the most grand and sumptuous court of the nineteenth century. The castle occupies a commanding position, standing upon a rocky hill some two hundred feet in height, rising abruptly above the marshy plain. It is encircled by a beautiful park composed of old cypress trees, draped in gray Spanish moss. We ascend the hill to the castle by a well-shaded road, formed of wood. On the side of this road, about half-way between base and summit, the tourist is shown a curious cave in which the Aztec kings were supposed to have deposited their treasures. In the grove of cypress at the base of the hill, one is shown a huge old tree, fifty feet in circumference, under which Montezuma I was wont to enjoy its cooling shade. There is plenty of evidence to show that when the Spaniard first came to the country, the plain of Anahuac was covered with a noble forest of these trees, together with oaks and cedars.

In the cypress grove, at the foot of the hill, I found, in the base of a rotton tree, a large colony of *Helix aspersa*, a land snail which was not

HELIX ASPERSA, MULL.

supposed, up to this time, to inhabit Mexico. Many of

them were found in trees twenty feet above the ground.
A little stream just outside of the grounds was tenanted
by innumerable specimens of *Physa osculans* and *Planorbis
tenuis*.

According to history, here stood the palace of the
ancient Aztec kings; and here has also been the abiding
place of the Mexican rulers, from the time of the first
Spanish viceroys to that of President Diaz.   At the base of
the hill, at the eastern foot, bursts forth the spring from
which the city is in part supplied with water, through the
San Cosme aqueduct, a heavy, arched structure, covered
with moss.   The castle is now used as the "West Point"
of Mexico, being the great military school wherein the
officers of the army are educated under the best foreign in-
structors.   Over three hundred students are quartered here,
representing the best families of Mexico.   The discipline,
however, is anything but good, and the drill exhibitions, in
the afternoon, would thoroughly disgust a West Pointer.

This spot is noted for a number of decisive historical
events.   Here, in 1847, the steep hill, though bravely de-
fended, was stormed by a mere handful of Americans in the
American-Mexican war.   In the rear of Chapultepec, and
less than two miles away, are the battle fields of Molino
del Rey and Churubusco, both victories for the Americans.
Both these battles, however, have been declared needless,
as the two positions could have been turned.   Near Molino
del Rey, the Mexicans have erected a monument to the
memory of their comrades.   The view from the lofty ram-
parts is the finest in the valley of Mexico.   From here the
valley of Anahuac is seen to be an elevated plain about
thirty-five by forty five miles in extent, its altitude being a
trifle less than eight thousand feet above the sea.   This
view embraces the City of Mexico, with its countless spires,
domes, and public buildings, the grand paseo leading to the

city, its widespread environs, the church of Guadalupe, the village-dotted plain, stretching away in every direction, the distant lakes burnished by the sun's rays, and the background toward the east of the two snow-clad mountains.

On the left of Chapultepec lies the suburban village of Tacubaya, where the wealthy citizens of the capital have their summer residences, many of which are very elegant. These are thrown open to strangers on certain days, to exhibit their collections of rare and beautiful objects of art. As the tourist leaves Chapultepec, by a narrow road winding through a grove of noble trees, attention is called to the ancient inscriptions upon the rocks at the eastern base of the hill near the roadside. They are in half relief, and are graven on the natural rock. As yet, no one has been able to decipher their meaning.

Of the twelve million people comprising the population of Mexico, about one-third are pure natives, one-sixth of the remainder Europeans, and the balance Mestizos, or half-breeds. The natives are of a brown or olive color, and are beardless, or nearly so; they are of medium height, stout or corpulent, have muscular thighs, a broad chest, and rather slender arms; they are not very strong, but are very enduring. The native retains his national dress, which consists of short, wide drawers of cotton cloth, or deer-skin, reaching to the knee, and a sort of frock of coarse woolen cloth, fastened around the hips by a belt; a straw hat and sandals complete his dress. The women wrap themselves twice around with a piece of woolen stuff, which is girded around the waist by a broad band, and reaches to her bare feet. In addition she wears a wide garment, called a *huipile*, closed on all sides, which reaches to her knees. Her hair is wound around her head in a roll and tied with a brightly colored ribbon, or hangs down in two plaits. Many wear

ear-rings and necklaces for ornaments. These natives (peons) are the working class of Mexico.

Our next class is the European, or Creole, the conquerors of Mexico. They are gentle and refined, yet passionate, and very courteous toward each other. They make delightful companions They are fond of gaming, and ardent admirers of the fair sex. Many of the women are exceedingly handsome, having dark eyes and hair. The women, however, are kept mostly shut up in the houses, and travellers rarely get a glimpse of them. They are excellent needle-women, and spend a great part of their time in this way. In their dress this class favor the French and conform to the latest Parisian styles. They wear the characteristic head-dress of the Spaniards, the *mantilla*.

The third race, the *Mestizos*, or mixed race, is the off-spring of white father and native mother. They are splendid horsemen, and seem to combine the best characteristics of the two races They wear, when dressed up, a white plaited shirt, wide trousers of white or colored material, fastened about the waist by a brilliant girdle, brown leather gaiters, and a broad felt hat, or *sombrero*, with a silver band about it. The *rancheros*, or peasants, are distinguished by the open trousers of leather, ornamented

AN ICE CREAM VENDER. with silver buttons, and white drawers underneath. A colored handkerchief about the neck and a *serape*, complete the outfit. The women wear loose, embroidered chemises, and a woolen skirt; they wear no stockings, although occasionally one is seen with slippers, and a *rebozo*, or a narrow, long shawl drawn over the head

PLATE XII.   MONTEZUMA'S TREE, CHAPULTEPEC.

and covering the bare arms. The *mestizos* constitute the majority of farmers (*rancheros*), and mule-drivers (*arrieros.*) They are very pleasant and are destined, some day, to rule Mexico.

Another type of the Mexicans are the *Leporos*. These are the worst type of Mexicans, combining, as they do, the worst vices known to man. They are black, have long and unkempt hair, and are alive with vermin; they are said to abhor water, seldom change their clothes, and are, upon the whole, disgusting and dangerous citizens of the Republic. At one time they were the terror of Mexico, but good government is now reducing their number greatly. They will steal, murder, pick your pocket, or commit any other of the acts known to creatures of the criminal class.

Another common Mexican sight is the honest *aquador*, or water-carrier, who, with his leathern armor and earthern jars, is seen on almost every Mexican street. All the water of the city is brought in aqueducts, and is to be obtained only at fountains. The aquador is then an absolute necessity, and is made welcome by all. He sells his jar of water for five cents, and seems to do a thriving business.

Animal life about the valley of Anahuac was very meagre. Of the Mollusca, *Helix aspersa, Succinca campestris* (Lake Texcoco), *Limnæa attenuata* (Lake Chalco), *Planorbis tenuis Physa osculans* (all lakes), *Valvata humeralis* (all lakes); of the reptiles and batrachians, *Sceloporus microlepidotus, S. scalaris, Eutænia insigniarum*, and *Amblystoma Mexicanum* were common. This last, commonly called the *axolotl* (pronounced ah-ho-lotl) is eaten by the poorer classes; its flesh is white and resembles that of an eel; it is quite savory and wholesome. Of birds, we saw few wild, save the ducks.

CHAPTER X.

On the 15th of April we left Mexico, by train, for Amecameca, from there to make the ascent of the volcano of Popocatepetl. After leaving the city, the road skirted the LaVega
canal, and soon struck across the plain bordering lakes Texcoco and Chalco. We soon passed the former on the left,
and the latter on the right, and then encountered an upward grade at the base of the mountains. Several stops
were made at pretty villages. At one of these villages we
were besieged by a multitude of beggars, the pest of Mexico. At five o'clock in the afternoon we reached Amecameca. This is a town of ten thousand inhabitants, situated
about 7,600 feet above the sea. In the center of the town
was the plaza, where a low, circular wall of stone enclosed
a small space, planted with flowers, a basin filled with
water flowing from a fountain in the center, and a few white
stone pillars supported a capital, which formed the entrance. Above these, and shading the garden, drooped a
number of green willows. The square surrounding this bit
of verdure was large, bounded on the west side, next the
railroad, by the Casa Municipal, and on the east by the
Cathedral, a large and well-preserved building. The streets
of the town diverged from this center, lined with low houses
of stone and adobe, of which the latter predominated,
roofed with rough shingles, spiked on with long wooden
pegs. Water from the mountains ran in little streams
through the streets, and was diverted by small gutters to
the houses for private use.

The view of the two mountains from this town was
grand, late in the afternoon. To the right and left, as far
as the eye could reach, extended the mountain chain, and

rising up in all their grandeur were the sister peaks. To the left was Ixtaccihuatl, its outline clearly defined against the sky, showing well the peculiar outlines which have caused it to be termed *La Mujer Blanco*, or the White Woman. On the right rose Popocatepetl, a great white dome. The effect of the sun's declining rays resting on the snow, the massiveness of the mountains, the swift gathering twilight and the tolling of the bells in the little chapel on the Sacro Monte, made an impression upon us which will never be effaced. I can conceive of no grander sight on earth than that afforded by this mountain scenery, as seen from this quaint town.

Next morning, at seven o'clock, we started for the volcano with five guides and carriers. The first part of our way wound among softly undulating slopes, yellow with barley, out of which projected here and there an ancient pyramid, planted with a crop also. By the roadside grew charming white thistles, and tall blue columbines. We crossed numerous small brooks and gorges. The aspect soon changed to that of an Alpine pasture. Here were grassy pastures, flowering mosses, and cattle feeding. Several small crosses were passed, indicating where some poor wretch had met a violent death, either from robbers or from some natural cause. Every few hundred feet we took the altitude with our aneroid barometer, for we had started out to take the altitude of this giant peak. Half way to the summit we obtained a magnificent view of the Mexican valley, looking down a wooded ravine. We soon entered the deep, solemn pine-woods, crossed a long ridge of land, and reached the Tlamacas ranch, 12,595 feet above the sea, where we were to spend the night.

The ranch consisted of three sheds, situated in a little opening in the forest, at the base of the peak. In one of the sheds a cheerful fire was burning, and preparations being

made for supper. Just before darkness settled down, I took
my gun and searched for birds. But few were found, and
those were the robin, bluebird, and several small warblers.
The same birds were observed on Orizaba at the same
relative height. A narrow platform covered with straw
served us for a bed and a saddle for a pillow, and with our
feet to the fire we fell asleep, to dream of snow-slides,
avalanches, and eruptions.

We left the rancho at five in the morning, on horseback, and rode three hours toilsomely over rocks of basalt
and black sand. The poor animals suffered painfully, but
we could not spare them, for we needed all our strength for
the final struggle. At a point called Las Cruces, where a
cross tops a ledge of black, jagged volcanic rock, we left
them and proceeded on foot. The view from this point in .
the ascent was fine. Across was the form of Ixtaccihuatl,
the White Woman, keeping us company in our ascent.
The valley of Mexico could be seen in one direction, the
valley of Puebla, and even the peak of Orizaba, 150 miles
distant, in the other. Against this vast territory, our men
and horses on the ledge of volanic rock at Las Cruces
seemed like pigmies. We soon felt the effect of the thin-
ness of the air, and were obliged to make frequent stops.
The cool snow line was soon reached, and here we sat down
and ate our lunch. Clouds presently filled up the valley
with a symmetrically arranged pavement.

At the snow-line more difficulties met us. We were
always slipping and falling in the snow, and blood-marks
were left frequently by our ungloved hands. Every step is
now a calculation and an achievement. One calculates
that he will allow himself a rest after ten, twenty, thirty or
more steps, and how glad he is, when that calculation has
been achieved, and he can rest for a few moments! The
snow here is not dangerous; there are no crevasses to fall

into, as in the Alps; it is only monotonous and fatiquing. The guides encouraged us with the adjuration, *"Poco à poco"* (little by little). Finally, with sore and aching limbs, we reached the crater, about eleven o'clock.

It seemed easy to topple over the crater walls into the terrific chasm below. There was no warm comf rt coming from the steam below. All was frigidly cold. A slope of black sand descended some fifty feet to an inner edge, broken by rocks of porphyry, where a sheer precipice dropped a thousand feet to the bottom of the crater. Jets of steam spouted from a dozen sulfataras, or sources from which the sulphur is extracted. The men who mine the sulphur (for Popocatepetl is a vast sulphur mine), live in caves at the bottom for a month at a time. They are lowered down by a windlass, or *Malacate*, and the sulphur is hoisted in bags by the same agent. The bags of sulphur are slid down a long groove in the snow to the neighborhood of the ranchero. A company, headed by General Sanchez Ochoa, the owner, has been formed to work the deposit more effectually, and to utilize the steam-power lying latent in the bottom of the crater. At the present moment the windlass was out of order, and we were not able to descend. The crater is nine hundred feet deep, and nearly one thousand feet wide at its greatest diameter. Its inner face is marked off in successive layers, representing the successive eruptions of the volcano.

After a great deal of dangerous and fatiquing climbing, we at length reached the actual summit of the mountain, ly· ing to the southwest, and overlooking the State of Morelos, seven hundred feet higher than our resting place on the edge of the crater. We were now 17,523 feet above the sea. From what we could learn we were the first persons to actually reach this highest point, although the Glennie brothers were said to have attained nearly the same height,

in 1827.   From this high elevation the view was of surpassing grandeur, taking in the country for hundreds of miles.
The view, however, was blurred and indistinct, on account
of the many clouds floating by.   Although the temperature
was only 45° Fahr., we did not suffer from the cold nearly
as much as we did on the snow-field below.   I suffered
from none of the symptoms which caused me to desist from
climbing on Orizaba, when within three hundred feet of the
summit.   Late in the afternoon we descended to Tlamacas,
spent one more night there, and the next day rode back to
Amecameca.

Of all the Mexican mountains, Popocatepetl has received the most attention, and has been ascended innumerable times.   The heights usually given to it I believe to be much too high,   Our records showed that
Orizaba, and not Popocatepetl, should be given first place
among the mountains of Mexico.   A short stop was made
at Amecameca, and then we returned to the City of Mexico.

On the 29th of April we left Mexico for Toluca, situated fifty miles from the city.   The trip to Toluca leads
through some of the grandest scenery in the country, as well
as taking the traveler over some of the most abrupt ascents
in Mexico.   After leaving the city, the road passes through
a district devoted to the cultivation of the Maguey, the
great pulque-producing plant.   There are two kinds of
this Maguey; the cultivated plant from which comes the
pulque, and one, which grows wild in the desert parts of the
country, and from which is distilled a coarse and highly
intoxicating drink called mescal.   But we are digressing;
let us speak of our journey to Toluca.   After passing
Tacubaya, the road began to steadily ascend, the line curv-
ing and twisting in and out to find a foothold upon the
mountain.   We passed Naucalpan and Rio Hondo, and
the ascent became very steep.   The bridge at Dos Rios was

soon passed, a structure two hundred feet long and ninety feet high. The line was now constantly ascending, circling about the mountains and passing over several small bridges. · Soon the passengers flocked to the rear platform to obtain a sight of the grand view afforded from this point. The glittering domes of the City of Mexico were seen in the distance; farther away, to the left, were seen the two large expanses of water, lakes Chalco and Texcoco, looking like burnished silver in the morning sunlight; far beyond, rising spectre-like, were the lonely peaks of Ixtaccihuatl and Popocatepetl. About them floated beautiful clouds, tinted in many colors by the sun's rays. Soon this was shut out by a tunnel, and for a time we saw nothing but cultivated fields and bare rocks. Here the natives had taken advantage of every spot, where there was a particle of earth, for agricultural purposes.

At *La Cima*, the summit, we reached the highest point, 10,000 feet above the sea. A little farther on we reached Salazar, built on a plain, where a halt was made for ten minutes. Here the air was quite crisp, and one felt the need of thick wraps. Here, also, the beggars again assailed us, and during the entire ten minutes we were not for a moment out of sight of one of these mendicants. One, in particular, had an old, battered violin. He was blind, and was led about by a boy, probably his son. One does not like giving to these beggars, since so many of them are frauds, and prey upon the travellers in this way as a regular means of livelihood. The descent into the Toluca Valley now began. On our right a clear, babbling brook was seen, the headwaters of the river Lerma; this stream went leaping and dancing down the mountain, the track crossing it in several places.

A short distance farther on, the beautiful valley of Toluca burst on our view. At the foot of the mountain the river Lerma was seen winding in and out; beyond was the green and fertile valley, dotted here and there with a hacienda; in the far distance was seen the great, black peak of the Nevado de Toluca, and at the foot of the mountain, . the white walls of Toluca.   Below us, and at our very feet, lay the little village of Ocoyoacac, a thousand feet below. Here the grade was terrific, and the line ran along in several horse-shoe shaped curves.   Finally, the last curve was made, and the train steamed across the broad and fertile valley of Toluca.   Very soon we passed a little village called *La Gran Ciudad de Lerma*, "The Great City of Lerma," which received its name in this way. During the 16th century, a band of robbers made their headquarters here and for a time were the terror of travellers and merchants, but one Marten Roelin de Varejon finally broke them up, in 1613, and in return for this good work the king granted him any favor that he should ask; and he asked that the town might be called "*La Gran Ciudad de Lerma.*" Soon the Lerma was crossed on a long bridge, the river here widening into a lake, and the line passed through large fields of corn and barley, and finally drew up in the dépot at Toluca.   From the dépot a tram-car was taken, and we were soon landed in front of the best hotel in the City of Toluca, *El Leon de Oro*, the "Lion of Gold," so named from a gilt Lion on the corner of the hotel.   Here we engaged rooms, a good wash was taken, supper eaten, and we were ready to inspect the city.

Toluca, the capital of the State of Mexico, is a well-built and thriving city, containing about twenty-five thousand inhabitants, and situated at an elevation of 8,600 feet above the sea.   The municipal buildings and state capital are said to be the finest in the Republic.   They face upon a delightful little plaza, which is adorned with several fine trees.   The town is one of the oldest in the country,

having been settled in 1533. Here activity and growth are
manifest on every side. It has two large theatres, a
spacious bull-ring, and a beautiful alameda, which is kept
in good condition. Here is situated the "Yale College" of
Mexico, the Instituto Literario, in which most of the leading men of Mexico were educated. The institution has a
large library and museum of natural history, together with
a well-appointed gymnasium. Here may be seen the best
and largest market in Mexico. It is all under cover, and
each article has its appropriate place of sale; vegetables,
fruits, meats, fish, flowers, pottery, baskets, shoes, and
sandals, form the chief articles of trade. On general
market day the spot is thronged with people from the surrounding country, dressed in their picturesque native costumes.

Near Toluca is the extinct volcano of the same name,
the crater of which forms a large lake, which is said to be
fathomless. On the second day after our arrival we essayed
its ascent. We left Toluca at 5:30 A. M., in a tram-car for
San Juan de las Hurtos. Here a guide and horses were
procured. The first stage of the ascent was very interesting. The day was very hot, and as we passed through the
woods everything was motionless, excepting the butterflies
which lazily fluttered about. The scene when crossing the
hills, behind San Juan, was most beautiful; the colors were
intense, the prevailing tint a dark green, the sky of a
deep blue. After passing through some cultivated fields,
we entered a forest, which in the grandeur of its parts
could not be exceeded. Early in the afternoon we arrived
at the base of the cone. Here we left the horses and
climbed up the steep and rocky crater-walls to the summit,
which commanded a grand view of the surrounding country.
The height of this mountain is not over 15,000 feet.

We spent the night at an Alpine-looking cottage sit-

uated in the midst of a pine forest, overlooking a deep ravine. Here we witnessed what very few tourists have the
good fortune to see—the native in his primative home, surrounded by his family. As we entered the hut, we beheld
an interesting scene. In the center of the hut a fire was
burning, and supported upon four stones was a large
earthern dish, upon which one of the native women was
frying tortillas. Another woman near by was busily engaged in grinding corn. Opposite her sat a woman nursing
a small child. In a corner was a goat, dog, and several
chickens. Several men and boys were standing near, all
busily engaged in watching the woman frying the tortillas.

One room serves the native for every purpose, and as
witnessed here, is often shared by pigs and poultry. The
natives do not eat meat half a dozen times a year. A few
wild fruits are added to their humble fare of tortillas, and
that suffices. A mat serves for a bed and a blanket for an
overcoat, and the native seems very content. They
supply the towns with poultry, charcoal, nuts, baskets,
pottery, and a few vegetables; often walking twenty-five or
thirty miles over hills and plains with a load of over a
hundred pounds on their backs, in order to reach a market
where a dollar, or at most two, is received for their two or
three days' journey. Most of the money made by the
natives is paid to the Catholic priests for pseudo-indulgen-
ces. On the following day we returned to the City of
Mexico.

The avifauna of Toluca was identical with that of
Popocatepetl. Warblers, robins, bluebirds, hawks, creep-
ers, and wrens predominated. Insects were also numerous,
but mollusks scarce.

On the 25th of April we again left the City of Mexico
for Amecameca, this time to ascend, and to take barometric

IXTACCIHUATL FROM AMECAMECA.

PLATE XIII.

measurements of Ixtaccihuatl. On the day following we started with three guides and carriers.

Our road was at first the same as that upon which we travelled on our way to Popocatepetl, but soon branched off to the left, and continued in a direction at right angles to that road. We soon entered a path bordered on either side by hedges of trees and shrubs, and with a viaduct on our right, through which a stream of clear water was running. The path was very stony and the riding uncom'ortable, but the scene about us interesting enough to compensate for this. The trees, in one spot, met above, forming a perfect arbor.

This path led to a wider one which crossed a stream, and then began to gently ascend. As we turned a corner, a beautiful field of green grass met our view on the left. The road soon became very steep, and difficult to ascend. By the roadside were many beautiful flowers, and we were tempted now and then to dismount and pick some of them. We soon entered a thick forest of pine and spruce, and for a time the scenery was much like that on Popocatepetl. When about half way up we passed, on our right, an extinct crater with shattered and jagged walls, looking as if the volcano had given one last eruption and blown the crater wall away. Birds were very numerous here, but were the same as those seen on the other mountains.

About the middle of the day we came to a position in the road which skirted a deep gorge on the left, and here the scenery was grand. Way off on the other side were huge, basaltic columns, standing out in bas-relief against the face of the lava field. The lava fields here were terraced, the terraces running back almost as far as the eye could reach. Over one part of this field a little stream was coursing, and as it reached the last terrace, dropped to the valley below in a beautiful waterfall several hundred feet in height. On the sides of the gorge, forests of pine and spruce were growing. All in all, this was about as wild and grand a scene as one could well imagine. At one point the path skirted the edge of the precipitous sides of the gorge, and was very narrow, the gorge on the left and a high wall of rock on the right.   •

We soon came in full sight of the cold, snow-capped peak, and dreary and desolate it did indeed look, but very grand and sublime in the light of the late afternoon. We now continued at right angles to the peak, and soon struck another patch of pine woods; crossed a little stream, descended the mountain a hundred feet or more, and prepared our camp in a sheltering cave, formed by the lava as it flowed from the crater. We were now at a height of 13,220 feet above the sea.

While supper was under way a thunder-storm came up, and we witnessed a royal battle of the elements. The thunder rolled among the crags of the mountain, and the lightning was almost blinding. The storm was so fierce that we ceased eating until the worst of it was over. In the midst of the storm a blinding flash descended, a deafning peal of thunder followed, and we beheld a large tree cut in twain by the lightning bolt. We could plainly see the electric bolt leave the clouds above and strike the tree, from which a little column of blue smoke arose, and the stricken half of the tree fell to the ground with a crash. After the storm was over, I descended to the stricken tree and found its stump black and burnt, and the tree cut in two as clean as if done with an axe.

A snowstorm followed this war of the elements, and we were treated to one of those rare sights, of seeing, far away, on the opposite mountain, the ground gradually become white, but not being able to discern a single flake in the air.

At an early hour on the day following, we mounted our horses to complete the ascent. The first part of the way was through a pine forest, but soon this was left behind, and we came to a rocky path where the progress was very difficult. Signs of a glacier in the vicinity were soon seen, for on either side of us were large moraines. Just before we reached the snow line the horses were left, and we continued on foot. Our path now ran along the crest of a ridge of lava jutting out from the mountain. On either side of us was a ravine, with a stream running down from the snow above. Very soon we came to the snow line, which was found to be a huge glacier, its surface quite smooth, and both difficult and dangerous to walk over. In various places there were glacial tables formed by the ice melting beneath a large stone, and leaving the latter suspended in mid air on a small pyramid of ice. These tables were continually falling over and being formed again. On every side deep fissures were seen cutting across the mountain in almost every direction.

The whole mountain was seen to be covered with a vast field of ice some 50 to 100 feet in depth, completely shrouding the summit. Across this we now directed our steps in a zig-zag course, to avoid the deep *barrancas* (crevasses). In many places the guides (but two of them made the ascent over the snow-fields with us) were obliged to cut steps for our feet. As we had experienced no difficulty on any of the other mountains from slipping, we had not brought foot swaths with us, and we now found that they would have lessened the danger to a great extent.

As we ascended higher the danger became more and more apparent, and in many places we climbed up with our faces almost touching the ice. Several bad slips were made, but we reached a point some seventy-five yards from the summit in safety. Here we found ourselves blocked by a large and impassable fissure, cutting directly across the mountain. The guides assured us that it would be impossible to reach the highest point, and we were therefore obliged to be content with our present elevation.

The aneroid indicated a height of 16,700 feet, which, added to the 75 yards (225 feet), made a total height of 16,925 feet. The thermometer registered 32°, and the air was exceedingly cold. From the summit we could see Popocatepetl off to the south, rising up like a great, white dome; way down the valley was the town of Amecameca, and over all floated a mass of white, fleecy clouds.

The descent to the cave was undertaken with but one mishap, and this was when one of our number slipped and nearly fell into a deep crevass. The cave was reached, however, without serious accident, and late in the evening we arrived in Amecameca. Ixtaccihuatl is the only one of the three giant volcanoes of Mexico, which partakes of the full dangers of Alpine climbing. In the Alps, travellers are tied to the guides by ropes, which prevents any one from being lost by falling into a crevass. Ladders and additional ropes are also carried. With us, however, nothing of the kind was taken, and so erroneous had been the reports concerning this mountain that foot-swaths and other needful articles were not taken, as they were not needed on the other mountains. The mountain bears evidence of having been, at one time, the giant of Mexican volcanoes, and was much higher than at present. The glacier has been named the " Porfirio Diaz Glacier" in honor of the President of the Mexican Republic. On our return to Mexico, I found that my eyes had been very badly affected by the dazzling sunlight on the ice and by the excessive mental strain, and for several days I was confined to the hotel on account of them.

The fauna and flora of Ixtaccihuatl was precisely that of Popocateptl. No mollusks were found, however, and but few birds seen.

CHAPTER XI.

APRIL 30th we again left the capital to explore the little known regions in the neighborhood of Patzcuaro, and the volcano of Jorullo. Our journey was by the same road which we took for Toluca. After leaving the latter place the road crossed the Toluca Valley, and passed through the Ixtlahuaca Tunnel. At Flor de Maria we secured a good dinner, costing seventy-five cents. From Flor de Maria we passed over a flat country, passed the gold workings of El Oro, at Tultenango, the silver district of Tlalpujahua, and entered Zopilote cañon, along the precipitous sides of which a space had been blasted just large enough for the track. Above us hung great masses of granite, rising up hundreds of feet; below dashed a beautiful stream, which in one spot formed a waterfall of great beauty. The down grade was very steep, and we entered the valley of Solis at good speed. This valley was covered with brilliantly colored flowers, presenting a very attractive scene. Maravatio, a town of five thousand inhabitants, was soon reached, after which we passed over a rather flat region, following the windings of the Lerma River. Toward Acambaro the scenery was very beautiful, the river being lined with graceful cypress trees, festooned with Spanish moss. From Acambaro we skirted the south shore of lake Cuitzeo for twenty miles. The scene here was very picturesque; the wall of rugged mountains in the distance, the broad sheet of water, dotted here and there with islands, green with a semi-tropical verdure, and the quaint costumes of the people, made a very pleasing picture. Darkness settled over us as we reached Morelia, capital of the State of Michoacan, called by its Spanish founders Valladolid, but renamed by the Mexicans, after the revolution of 1810, Morelia, in honor of the patriot Morelos. This city is well known as being one of the most beautiful of the Republic.

At 10:15 P. M. we reached the little dépot at Patzcuaro, situated about two miles from the town, which was reached by a rambling diligence. The road from the dépot to the town was paved with small boulders, which nearly shook our coach to pieces. No sort of torture could be greater than this, in the shaky old stage coach. We arrived at the Fonda Concordia about an hour and a half later, and secured a good room, and also a cup of coffee, an omelet, and some fruit.

Patzcuaro is situated two hundred and seventy-four miles from Mexico,—at an elevation of 7,200 feet above the sea,—and lies in a hollow, two miles from the lake of the same name, which is only visible from certain elevations in the town. If it lay in full view of the lake, it would have one of the most beautiful situations possible. The town is primitive and solid, and as yet very little affected by intercourse with the outside world. It has a large plaza, shaded by mountain ash trees, and surrounded by arcades and colonnades, in which are the shops of the merchants. The roofs of the town are tiled, and most of the houses, being of one story, have projecting cornices of wood, with supporting beams. The town is irregular and hilly, but all paved very roughly. On the highest elevation is a plaza,— the third in the town,—planted with noble trees, and fronted by the grim walls of an old monastery. Every· where are signs of a former haughty ecclesiastical denomination, now scattered and in contempt. In the lower plaza is situated the market, where, as is common with Mexican markets,—everything manufactured in the immediate neighborhood can be purchased. It has been prophesied that at no distant day, this town will be one of the most favored tourist resorts in Mexico.

The lake of Patzcuaro is noted for its beauty, even though situated in a district where nature has excelled herself in the production of magnificent scenery. At this high altitude, among the mountains of the ancient Tarascan empire, is found this lovely sheet of water, some twenty miles long by ten wide, and interspersed with islands,

SCENE IN THE MARKET.

most of which are inhabited by a hardy race of fishermen. The water of the lake is very clear, and of unknown depth. The sportsman can find here many species of water fowl common to the North, besides many other varieties.

From the top of a hill, three-quarters of a mile from the town, a magnificent view of the lake was obtained. The hills surrounding the lake were under cultivation, dotted here and there by a little village, of which as many as sixteen could be counted. The lake can be compared with but one locality with which I am acquainted,—that of Narragansett Bay in Rhode Island.

Late in the forenoon I took my gun, and in company with Prof. H. visited the lake to see what it contained in the faunal line. We procured a boat and a pilot, and started to survey the shores. After poling through a small patch of clear water, we struck into a clump of reeds which lined the shore for some distance. In these reeds I shot several specimens of the Bi colored Blackbird. As we emerged from the thickest of the reeds, I noticed a flock of ducks resting quietly upon the water. Motioning to the native to go ahead slowly, I cocked both barrels of my gun and just before the boat emerged from the reeds, let drive both barrels at them.

Just as I was about to order the boatman to paddle toward the spot where the dead ducks lay, I saw a single Ring-neck, for such these ducks were, winging his way toward me. Unsuspicious of danger, he drew near, and even as I raised my gun to my shoulder, he merely swerved a trifle to one side. As I fired, he fell with a resounding splash into the water.

Our boatman now turned toward the west, and paddled toward an island some distance away. On the lake we saw numbers of canoes plying too and fro between the north and south shores. What was very peculiar about these canoes, was the fact that they were built on almost identically the plan of those used by the natives of the South Sea Islands, and I could almost imagine myself among those famous islands, as canoe after canoe was rapidly paddled across the lake. The boatmen rest on their knees in the bottom of the canoes, and use the paddle alternately with the right and left hand. One of these large canoes, I noticed, was manned entirely by women, who seemed to be able to propel the canoe along quite as rapidly as their stronger brothers and husbands.

I soon caught sight of a stake ahead, upon which were resting a number of birds. We slowly approached, and just as they started to fly I hastily singled out one and fired, bringing him to a stand in a hurry. It proved to be the Least Bittern (*Botaurus exilis*), and was a valuable addition to our bag. A flock of ducks, probably Ring-necks, came over at this moment, and I let drive two barrels at them, but missed. A few hundred yards further on we came to the island. As we approached, a commotion was observed in the water, and a snake was seen to glide swiftly and noiselessly away. I quickly shot it; on picking it up we found it to be a large species of water-snake (*Eutænia insigniarum*).

As we pushed our boat in among the reeds bordering the island, a great commotion was created in the water, and a number of these snakes were seen to swim away. The boat was securely fastened to the shore, and we started to explore this small island. This was of but small extent, containing less than half an acre; it was once used as a place of worship, and the remains of a church could still be seen. It was covered with low bushes and cacti; among the roots of the cacti I found several dead shells of *Glandina*, and from the rocks bordering the lake I picked several shells, but not a living thing was to be found on the island except the snakes, shells, and a single lizard, which was seen running up the trunk of a tree.

Among the shells found in the lake were many speci-

 mens of *Physa osculans* (this proved to be a new variety and was named var. *Patzcuarensis* by Mr. H. A. Pilsbry), a handsome little *Valvata*

PHYSA OSCULANS. (*V. humeralis*) and a number of

PLANORBIS TENUIS.

specimens of *Planorbis tenuis, Phil., var. Boucardi,* C. & F. On our return I shot a handsome specimen of the White-faced Glossy Ibis (*Plegadis guarauna*),and an American Coot.

But a single day was spent in Patzcuaro, where we se-cured horses and a mozo, or servant, and started on our journey to the volcano of Jorullo. We left Patzcuaro early in the morning, by a steep path which led into a dusty road. For several miles the road was over a rolling country, well under cultivation. About fifteen miles from Patzcuaro I shot a couple of birds, whose habits resembled those of the robin. They were the *Chamaeospiza torquata,* a somewhat rare and very interesting bird. It very much resembles a tanager, and was at one time described as such by no less an authority than Mr. Lawrence (Am. Lyc., N. Y., viii, 120).

Now and then we met a caravan of burros carrying
large sacks on their backs, and driven by half-naked natives.
Occasionally, a whole family was seen, consisting of father,
mother, several grown up children, and one or two younger
ones. Late in the afternoon we reached Ario de Rosales,
a small village of a few hundred inhabitants, where we spent
the night. Next morning we again set out, and about nine
o'clock reached a large pine forest, bordering the valley
in which was situated the volcano. The view from this
point was grand in the extreme; the great plateau upon
which we had been travelling ended here, and dropped, perpendicularly, into a valley fifteen hundred feet below, leaving a bare and ragged mountain wall on the east side of the
valley. To the right was seen Jorullo, standing out of
the plain, a great, black mass. In the valley were seen
plantations, looking beautifully fresh and green, and way
off in the distance the Sierra Nevada range of mountains
bordering the Pacific Coast. The scene was one of those
grand productions of nature which defied the pen to
describe, and which only the brush of the artist could
adequately picture.

As we descended into the valley the change from the
tierra templada to that of the *tierra caliente*, or hot lands,
was very marked. Pines gave way to palmettos, papaws,
and other trees of the tropics. Loose thatched huts were
seen in place of the tight, mud-plastered huts of the temperate climes. The little village of La Playa was soon
reached and we were cordially received by the major domo,
who had been advised of our coming. This little village was
very unique, and was composed of a single, large house, in
which lived the major domo and where all the supplies of
the village were kept, which was surrounded by a number of
thatched huts. The whole population did not number over
one hundred, and was composed almost entirely of natives,

IN THE VALLEY OF JORULLO.

PLATE X V

many of whom could not speak Spanish. Here we were
 compelled to eat our meals with
our fingers, with what little aid we
could get from a wooden spoon.
Our fare consisted of fried eggs,
beans, tortillas, and coffee, minus
milk. In the thick woods about
the valley were numbers of beautiful
birds. Here I saw, for the first
time, the handsome blue macaws,
and a single toucan of large size.
They flew very high, however, and
I was not able to shoot one. I
was able to shoot a Cassin's King-

TYRANNUS VOCIFERUS SW. bird, Crested Cassic, a Western
Lark Sparrow, and a strange woodpecker; these, together
with a small ground squirrel, were the only specimens
obtained.

On the following morning we started on horseback for
the volcano of Jorullo. Our road lay over an old lava
stream, and was covered with large and small blocks of
lava. The base of the cone was reached in about an hour,
and here the horses were left and the rest of the ascent ac-
complished on foot. The surface of the cone was covered
with scoria and the ascent was difficult, dangerous, and
fatiguing. The rim of the crater was reached at last,
and the view afforded fully recompensed us for the
exertion. Inside the crater steam was seen issuing from
several vent holes, and light detonations could be heard
occasionally. On the north, south and west sides, the walls
of the crater were intact, but on the eastern side the wall
had been broken away, and the lava had flowed out in a
great stream, which reached far down the valley. The
temperature of one of the vent holes in the crater registered

150° Fahr., and the ground beneath our feet was so hot that
we could scarcely bear our feet on it for a moment.   The
general form of the cone was that of a parallelogram; the
broken side on the east, however, had so destroyed its
outlines that it was difficult to determine just what had
been its original shape.   Jorullo erupted in September,
1759, converting what was a fertile plain, covered with

VOLCANO OF JORULLO.

sugar-cane, into a black desert, or malpays.   Two small riv-
ers were totally absorbed, and disappeared.   At the present
time (1895) Jorullo is showing signs of great activity, and,
it is not at all impossible for it to again erupt, as in 1759.
Should this happen, the village of La Playa and the numerous haciendas scattered about over the valley would be destroyed.

About noon we left La Playa and retraced our steps
to Patzcuaro, arriving there the second day after leaving
La Playa.   The night of the second day of our journey I
shall not soon forget.   Our way led over a rough mountain
path, cut up by innumerable barrancas.   The scene by
moonlight was grand; the sky was clear, and the moon
shone brightly, casting weird shadows here and there.   The
forest stood out black against the horizon, and to add to

the effect, not a leaf was stirring, nor a sound to be heard. We had arrived in Patzcuaro on the Mexican Fourth of July, the holiday known to them as the Cinco de Mayo,—the Fifth of May,—to commemorate their victory over the French at Puebla during the French Intervention. Horns were blowing, cannons firing, and every demonstration of pleasure exhibited. Everybody was in holiday attire, the market place was filled with people, and the town generally had an air of great rejoicing. At 12:30 A. M. we rode on horseback to the dépot, and at 3 o'clock took the train for Mexico.

CHAPTER XII.

MAY 9th we again set out, this time to visit Yautepec, where there was said to be good fields for study in Geology. The road,—the Morelos Railroad by the way,—was the same one over which we travelled to Amecameca. At the latter place the road passes along the base of the famous Sacro Monte. This hill rises abruptly from the plain; a shrine is placed here on its summit, around which all manner of legends are entwined. There is an image of the dead Christ preserved, which was placed there by Fray Martin, in 1527. For several centuries, annual pilgrimages have been made to this sacred spot, and there is reason to believe that all these rites and customs antedate christianity, from the fact that they are participated in almost wholly by natives.

From Amecameca to Ozumba the road was on a slightly descending grade, through a fertile valley, with the peaks of the snow-capped mountains on the left. In the fields were seen several natives using the ancient plough of wood, drawn by oxen. At Ozumba the steep descent began; in many places the track could be seen three times in the same place, where it doubled and twisted to obtain a foothold on the steep side of the mountain. At Nepantla we passed the up train, and here were seen several cages of beautiful birds in the dépot. At Cuautla we encountered, after passing through a most desolate region, a spot which seemed like an oasis in the midst of a desert, it was so green and fertile. At 3:45 we arrived in Yautepec and secured accommodations in the Zaragoza hotel.

Yautepec is a picturesque little town, situated in the midst of a barren volcanic region. The streets are narrow and crooked, and the houses are built of stone, with tiled roofs, as in many of the other towns we had visited. The streets are paved with cobble-stones in a very uneven manner, and resemble some of the streets in Philadelphia in this respect. In the center of the town, near the river, is a good sized plaza, with a fountain in the center. There are stone benches about the square, and a band stand near the fountain Flower-beds add to the beauty and picturesqueness of the square. The buildings facing the plaza are mostly used for government purposes, and are not very imposing. A river runs through the town, and is crossed by a stone bridge of good construction. Near the bridge a number of women and men were bathing, the men on one side and the women on the other, both destitute of bathing clothes. It seemed rather strange to us, but was the custom, and, of course, aroused no curiosity among the inhabitants. A little way from the river is a large hill, called Cerro de Calveria, which is used as a place of pilgrimage by the inhabitants. There is a cross on its summit, and a stony path leads to it, over which the devout natives crawl on their hands and knees.

The banks of the river were lined with thick vegetation, in which I distinguished the trees of the anona, date palm, banana, and orange. The ash, tepiguaje, and parotilla were very commonly seen. From the summit of the Cerro de Calveria a magnificent view was obtained; at our feet lay the town of Yautepec, with its curious winding streets and queer houses; on the outskirts were seen beautiful, green gardens of orange and banana trees laid out in squares, and mixed in here and there were mangos, anonas, and many other fruit trees of the tropics; in the background rose the black and rugged peaks of the broken-down volcanoes, and behind these rose the loftly mountain range of the Mexican Plateau, surmounted by the glistening white dome of Popocatepetl, piercing the clouds; through the center of the town flowed the little, nameless river, flowing through a beautiful gorge bordered by luxuriant vegetation. All about us were old volcanic cones, the only green and fertile spot to be seen being the town of Yautepec We could see that the lava streams which flowed from Popocatepetl on the southeast were very large, and must have reached nearly, or quite, to the Gulf. The small cones about the base of the plateau looked broken and jagged, as though a tremendous explosion had taken place.

Molluscan life was here quite abundant, and I was fortunate enough to discover a new species of *Potamopyrgus,*

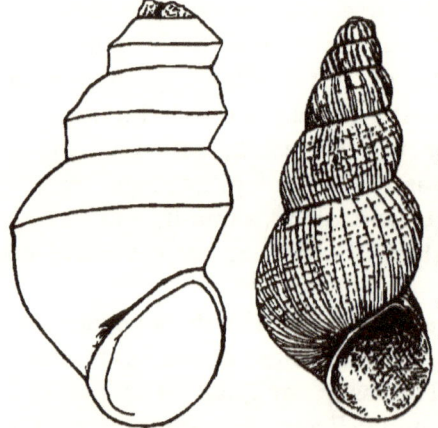

which Mr. H. A Pilsbry has called *P. Bakeri* in honor of its discoverer. It was found in the little river which runs through the town.   Such forms as *Pupa servilis, P Contracta, Stenopus elegans, Planorbis parvus,* and *Physa osculans* were quite numerous. Birds were not numerous.

POTAMOPYRGUS BAKERI, PILSBRY.

The town was built upon Cretaceous limestone, and several mountain ridges could be seen to the southwest. The whole plateau, and the numerous small cones in the neighborhood, seemed to have been thrust up through this deposit. At the bridge crossing the river a curious fact was observed; the rock on the left bank was composed of limestone, while that on the opposite side was composed of lava, the river flowing between the two deposits.

At night we had a concert of frogs, which made most

extraordinary noises. There were three kinds, which could frequently all be heard at once. One of these made a noise something like what one would expect a frog to make, namely, a dismal croak, but the sounds uttered by the others were like no sound I ever heard an animal make before. A distant railway-train approaching, and a black-smith hammering on an anvil, were the only noises with which I could compare them.

Two days were spent in this interesting town, when we returned to Mexico and from thence to Zumpango, to visit the Nochistongo cut. Here the English engineering firm of Reed & Campbell were engaged in digging a huge tunnel to drain the valley of Mexico, and especially lake Zumpango, whose waters had long threatened the destruction of the City of Mexico. This tunnel was to be nine and one-half miles in length, and at an average depth of two hundred and fifty feet. The tunnel was to connect with the *Tajo de Nochistongo* (the cut before referred to), and the waters carried from thence into the Montezuma River, which empties into the Gulf of Mexico. This great canal was commenced in 1601 for the proper drainage of the valley of Mexico. It varied in width from two hundred and eighty to six hundred and thirty feet, with a depth of from one hundred and fifty to one hundred and ninety-six feet. The Mexican government endeavored to utilize it for drainage purposes a few years ago, but the attempt was a failure, and the present company were using it as a terminus for the tunnel.

The City of Mexico is much below the level of several of the lakes, the waters of lakes Chalco and Yochimilco being ten, and those of lake Zumpango twenty-five feet above the city. In order to save the city, which has been twelve times wholly and partially inundated, it was decided to divert the waters of Zumpango into the river Montezuma, as described above. For three hundred years the sewers of the city have attempted to discharge into lake Texcoco, but the refuse matter 'is continually floating back again, and so the filth of nearly five hundred years is accumulated beneath the streets of the city. It is to assist this drainage, also, that these works are being carried on.

Two days were spent at Zumpango, and a good deal of information gained concerning the geological formation of the valley. On our return to Mexico we passed the little town of Popotla, in which is the famous Arbol de la Noche Triste, the "Tree of the Sorrowful Night," under which Cortez was said to have wept when driven from the City of Mexico. This was an old cypress with blasted, jagged limbs, and black trunk. It was surrounded by a railing to keep curiosity hunters from carrying the tree away.

On the twenty-fifth of May we left the City of Mexico, for the last time, for Veracruz, by the way of Tehuacan,

TREE OF THE SAD NIGHT.

where we wished to visit the onyx quarries. As we sped along the shore of lake Texcoco, the two mountains, Popocateptl and Ixtaccihuatl, stood out bold and clear as though bidding us farewell. About noon we arrived at Esperanza, where we change from steam to mule traction for Tehuacan. These tram-cars were very peculiar, being divided into compartments like an English railway carriage. The line ran between two ranges of limestone hills, and was continually descending. As we got deeper among the hills palmetto and freycinetta trees appeared, and the Spanish bayonet, that plant with the terrible sharp-pointed leaves, was seen in clusters here and there. A portion of the way we bordered a deep and picturesque cañon on the left, the track here running close to the base of the mountain on that side. At 5:30 P. M. we entered Tehuacan.

The town seemed to be about as large as that of Orizaba. The buildings, however, were more tastefully built, and had considerably more ornamentation. In the center was the usual plaza. This was neat and trim, and flowers were more numerous than in any previous town visited. It was now tenanted principally by a flock of grackles, who were making the air musical with their chattering. The churches here were of a superior quality as regarded architecture; one, in particular, had a dome built of tiles in the form of a mosaic. The bells were also wonderfully sweet and silvery in tone, and it was a pleasure to hear the chimes peal forth their notes on the still evening air. Altogether, Tehuacan had an air of freshness about it which was very pleasing.

On the morning after our arrival we procured horses and a mozo, and started to visit the onyx quarries, situated near the village of San Antonio. My horse, unfortunately, was not as good as my companions' who soon distanced me, and I was compelled to visit the quarries alone. The road was over an undulating country, sandy, and in many places thickly covered with bushes, with here and there a large tree. Cacti were everywhere abundant, growing in immense masses, having great woody stems as thick as a man's body, and were quite a novel feature in the landscape. Many of them were of the branched candelabrum form, and twenty to thirty feet in height. Other kinds were also abundant, some of them growing very low and shaped like a barrel. By the roadside several varieties of minerals cropped out, and quite a collection was obtained.

About noon I reached the little village of San Antonio, situated in a ravine, and on the opposite side of the ravine the marble quarry was seen. The village consisted of but a half dozen huts, and the inhabitants scampered out of sight as soon as they saw me. The onyx quarries were just outside of, and several hundred feet above, the village. Here were lying about huge pieces of onyx several feet square. One block was fully twelve feet long, and a foot and a half in thickness. The whole mountain seemed to be a mass of this mineral, and the road was paved with polished marble made bright by the constant travel over it. This onyx was a crust, interbedded with the distinctive limestone. Hippuritc fossils were found above and below, which determined its position. The beds were several feet in thickness

The absence of animal life about these mountains was remarkable. Scarcely a bird was to be seen, and they were, curiously enough, mostly birds of prey. A few ground-colored lizards and a cotton-tail rabbit were the only other animals seen. On the following day we left Tehuacan for Veracruz.

CHAPTER XIII.

MAY 28th we left Veracruz for Jalapa. From Veracruz to San Juan, sixteen miles, we passed through a most
delightful tropical country, the road running through an
almost impenetrable jungle. Birds here were numerous,
but I was not able to identify them.

We reached San Juan by train, where we changed to
mule traction. The road was very tortuous, winding up
long hills and down steep gulches. Our route was through
the old national road by way of Cerro Gordo. It was at
this hamlet, consisting of a few mud huts, that General
Scott, in 1847, outflanked and defeated the Mexican army
under Santa Ana. Jalapa,—pronounced Halápa,—is situated about sixty miles northwest of Veracruz, and is used
by the people of the latter city as a sanitarium to escape
from the ravages of yellow fever. Its situation is very
salubrious, as it is located some four thousand feet above
the sea coast.

Jalapa has a population (permanent) of some fourteen
thousand. It contains a large cathedral and numerous
churches, once handsome structures, but now fallen into
decay. The town is situated on the hill of Macuiltepec,
and many of the streets are therefore very steep, and the
scenery really beautiful. The low stone houses are perched
on the hillsides, and the streets are irregular. Among the
many attractions of Jalapa, those of its beautiful women
and lovely flowers are probably the widest known. In its
gardens may be gathered the fruits of almost every zone.
Here grows the aromatic vanilla plant, which is indiginous
and grows wild in abundance in the forest; it is a great
source of income to the inhabitants. The plant requires

only shade and moisture, and the climate does the rest.   The fiowers of this plant are of a greenish-yellow, touched here and there with white.   The pods grow in pairs and are about as large around as one's little finger, and six inches long.   The pods are green at first and gradually grow yellow, and then to brown, as they become fully ripe. They are carcfully dried in the sun, being touched during the process with palm oil which gives them a soft, glossy effect when they reach the consumer's hands.   The quantity shipped from Jalapa is very large, and proves an important source of revenue.   It is said that the Totonacs, who dwelt in the region, cultivated this plant, the Aztec nobles being very fond of the fragrant vegetable.   Another notable plant which grows here, and from which the town derives its name, is the jalap, an important drug in our medical practice.   Near Jalapa are seen the ruins of an ancient town, the builders of which must have attained to a high degree of civilization.   They resemble the ruins of Yucatan, and are supposed to have been built at about the same time.

The atmosphere of Jalapa is always humid, and the town is often overshadowed by clouds which come up' from the Gulf of Mexico, heavy with moisture to be precipitated in the form of rain.   A sort of "drizzle" prevails here most of the time.

In the center of the town is situated the old convent of San Francisco, supposed to have been erected by Cortez.   It was also the birthplace of General Santa Ana, the most noted of Mexican soldiers of fortune.   His neglected hacienda is pointed out to all tourists.   No man living had a more checkered career, now falling from position only to reach a greater elevation, from which to be ignominiously hurled.

The natives go about during the day only half clad,

both men and women exposing a large portion of the bare body to the atmosphere; at night, however, it was observed that both sexes protected their necks and shoulders with wraps; the men winding their woolen serapes over their necks and the lower parts of their faces, and the women covering theirs with their reboses. The change of temperature soon after sunset and in the early mornings, as compared with the rest of the day, is very decided throughout Mexico. Foreigners who follow the native customs avoid taking cold, while those who do not, suffer for their heedlessness.

A peculiarity was observed at Jalapa. While most of the women in Mexico are dark-hued, yet a large number of those one meets in Jalapa are .decidedly blondes, having light hair with blue eyes, and possessing as blooming complexions as any of our country girls in the States.

Like all Spanish cities, the windows of the dwellings are secured by a screen of iron bars, and many fronts,

where the house is of two stories in height, have also little balconies. These balconies are much in use by lovers. A Mexican never goes about a courtship in an open, straightforward manner, but on the contrary he forms cunning schemes for meeting his fair inamorata, and employs ingenious subterfuges to gain a stolen interview. He tells his passion not in words, but with profound sighs and significant glances as he passes her

MEXICAN COURTSHIP.

balcony, while she, although perfectly understanding his pantomine, assumes the most profound innocence. Finally, after a good deal of pretentious pantomime, the fair señorita appears to realize the purport of all his worry, and seems gradually to yield to his silent importunities. This is called "Playing the Bear." There is also the language of the fan, of the flowers, of the fingers, all of which are pressed into the service of the young couple. A small book is sold in the stores of Mexico which contains a printed code of the significance of certain flowers, a "dumb alphabet" for the fingers, and the meaning of the motions of the ever ready fan. The gradual opening of a fan signifies reluctant forgiveness, a rapid flirt scorn, an abrupt closing signifies vexation, and the striking of it with the palm of the hand expresses anger. In short, the fan can be more eloquent than words if in the hands of a Mexican señorita. This, however, is only preliminary. All parents are presumed to be absolutely opposed to all lovers' wishes, and great diplomacy is consequently required. This game often continues for a twelvemonth before anything is consummated. The charm in this kind of courting seems to be in its secrecy and difficulties, both real and assumed.

Between the lofty peak of Orizaba and the Cofre de Perote there exists many traces of a very numerous population, which must have occupied the country long previous to the time of Cortez. This locality is abundantly supplied with water, is fertile to an extraordinary degree, and possesses an exceptionally healthy climate. The remains of stone dwellings are to be found here, which must have laid here ruined for many centuries. Huge oak trees, four feet in diameter, are found growing among the ruins, proving their age. A number of stone pyramids have been found here also, some ten, others fifty feet in height; several of these have been opened and found to contain skeletons and highly decorated rooms. Why this locality is not used for agricultural purposes is a puzzle.

On our return to Veracruz, we stopped a couple of days at the little village of San Juan. The village consisted of ten or fifteen huts, and its population was not over seventy-five or one hundred. It was situated, however, in the midst of a dense tropical jungle, and on this account was of great interest to us. On leaving the village we walked along a straight country road, constructed above the level of the surrounding land. It had low swampy ground on one side, and the other was high enough to be quite dry. Leaving the road and turning into another, we arrived at a part where the lofty forest towered up like a wall, five or six yards from the path, to the height of a hundred feet. The trunks of the trees were only seen partially here and there, nearly the whole frontage from ground to summit being covered with a drapery of creeping plants, all of the most vivid green; scarcely a flower was to be seen, except in some places a solitary scarlet blossom, set in the green mantle. The low ground on the borders, between the forest wall and the road, was encumbered with a tangled mass of shrubby vegetation. About this spot numerous butterflies were sporting in the warm sunlight.

A mile further on the character of the woods changed, and we found ourselves in the primeval forest. Here the land was rather more elevated; the many swamp plants with their long and broad leaves were wanting, and there was less underwood, although the trees were wide apart. In almost every hollow was a little brook, whose cold, dark, leaf stained waters were bridged over by tree trunks. The ground was carpeted by Lycopodiums—those beautiful fern-like mosses—and was also encumbered with masses of vegetable débris and a thick coating of dead leaves. Fruits of many kinds were scattered about, among which were many kinds of beans, some of the pods being six

inches long, flat and leathery in texture ; others were hard
as stone.   What attracted our attention chiefly were the
colossal trees.   The general run of trees had not remarkably thick stems ; the great height to which they grew without throwing out a branch was a much more noticeable
feature than their thickness ; but at intervals of a rod or
two a veritable giant towered up to a height of a hundred
and fifty feet.

Birds here were very numerous.   Beautiful cassiques
were continually flying about from tree to tree, uttering
their peculiar note, which sounded like the creaking of a
rusty hinge.   On almost every tall tree we saw a hawk or
buzzard.   Pretty paroquets were very plentiful, and it
was amusing to watch the activity with which they climbed
about over the trees, and how suddenly and simultaneously
they flew away when alarmed.   Their plumage was so
nearly the color of the foliage that it was sometimes impossible to see them, though one might have seen them
enter a tree, and hear them twittering overhead, and, after
gazing until one's patience was exhausted, see them fly off
with a scream of triumph.   The Molluscan genera *Physa*
and *Planorbis* were very common.

Late in the afternoon of the second day we returned to
Veracruz, and secured accommodations in the Hotel Uni-
versal, fronting the Plaza Major.

CHAPTER XIV

THE City of Veracruz is said to be one of the most unhealthy spots on this continent, and the vomito holds high carnival six months of the year, claiming a large number of victims annually. The yellow fever makes its appearance in May, and is generally at its worst in August and September, when it creeps upwards towards Jalapa and Orizaba, although it has never been known to exist, to any grert extent, in either of these places. In summer the streets of Veracruz are almost deserted except by the buzzards and stray dogs, and at such times the city is called, very appropriately, *Una ciudad de los muertos* (a city of the dead).

A large share of the business of the city is carried on by French and German residents, who have become acclimated. Many of the merchants of the city keep up a permanent residence at Jalapa to escape this dreaded enemy. It is said that when a person has once contracted the disease, and recovered from it, he is presumed to be exempt from a second attack; this is a rule, however, not without an exception. It is singular that the climate of the Gulf side of the peninsula should be so fatal to human life, while the Pacific side, situated in the same latitude, is so very healthy. The French army had reason to remember Veracruz, for the fever decimated their ranks to the number of four thousand men.

The city is said to be more or less oriental in aspect. Everything is seen through a lurid atmosphere. Groups of mottled church towers surmounted by glittering crosses; square, flat-roofed houses; a long reach of hot sandy plain on either side relieved by a few palm trees; and rough fortifications—these make up the picture of the flat shore. There are no suburbs, the dreary, sandy desert creeping up close to the city. In the background, however, the monotonous scene is relieved by the Sierra Madre range of mountains, culminating in the peak of Orizaba. .

The long, straight, narrow streets are laid out with great uniformity, and cross each other at right angles, the monotony being broken by green blinds opening on the little balconies, which are shaded by awnings. The area of the city is not over sixty acres, the town being built in a very compact manner. The streets are crowded in' business hours; mule carts, porters, half-naked water-carriers, natives, negroes, and active civilians, besides a few military officers, are seen jostling each other. In the plaza pretty flower-girls mingle with fruit venders, lottery-ticket sellers, and here and there a half-tipsy seamen on shore-leave from the shipping in the roadstead.

The Plaza de la Constitucion is small in extent, about two hundred feet square, but it is very attractive, having a bronze fountain in its center, the gift of Carlotta, the unfortunate wife of Maximilian. In the evening the plaza is lighted by electricity. The plaza is ornamented with many lovely tropical flowers, cocoanut palms, and fragrant roses. On a pleasant evening it is amusing to watch the young people in shady corners making love, not, however, the legitimate Romeo and Juliet sort observed in Jalapa.

There are but few places of interest in Veracruz after visiting the governor's palace, the plaza, the alameda, with its fine array of cocoa-palms, the custom-house, the public library, and the large church fronting the plaza. This latter, while an imposing structure, will not compare well with the cathedrals in the other cities visited. One street, called the Street of Christ, leads to the Campo Santo, or burial ground, where nature has adorned the neglected city of the dead with beautiful and fragrant flowers.

The city houses are built of coral limestone, stuccoed. The corals are identical with species now found living in the harbor. The interior arrangements are like those else-where described. The narrow streets are kept scrupulously clean, are paved with cobble-stones, and have a gutter running down the middle. The garbage wagons make their rounds twice daily, gathering up all the refuse mat-ter. There is another keen-eyed scavenger, however, which is much more effectual and thorough than these garbage gatherers; these are the dark-plumed buzzards, or zopilo-tes (*Catharista atrata*), who are always on the alert to pick up and devour refuse matter of any sort found in the streets or about the houses. They even fight among themselves for coveted pieces of garbage on top of the wagons, and frequently the wagon will be half emptied

before it reaches the dumping place. They are wisely protected by law, and a fine imposed for killing them. Clouds of these birds may be seen roosting upon the eaves of the houses, the church belfries, and all exposed balconies. As the sun sets, the vultures flock to the domes of the churches, until the latter are literally black with them. There is one

ZOPILOTE.

mystery in regard to these birds which naturalists are trying to solve, namely, their breeding place. No one knows where they go to build their nests and rear their young.

Although Veracruz has suffered more than almost any other capital from bombardments, ravages of bucca-neers, hurricanes, fevers, and changes of rulers, yet it is still a prosperous city. A brief glance at its past history shows us that in 1568 it was in the hands of pirates, that in 1683 it was sacked by buccaneers, and was devastated by a conflagration in 1618. In 1822--23 it was bombarded by the Spaniards, who still held the castle of San Juan de la Ulua. In 1838 it was attacked by a French fleet, and in 1847 was bombarded by the American forces. In 1856 it was nearly destroyed by a hurricane, and in 1859 civil war decimated the town and fortress. From 1861 to 1867 it was in the hands of the French and Imperialists. From that time, however, it has enjoyed a period of quiet and a large share of commercial prosperity.

Veracruz, though at present the principal seaport of the Republic, is without a harbor worthy of the name, being situated on an open roadstead and offering no safe anchorage among its shoals, coral reefs, and surfs. It is not safe for vessels to anchor within half a mile of the shore. A cluster of dangerous reefs, including the Island of San Juan, form a slight protection from the open Gulf, although this is sometimes more dangerous than an open roadstead. A sea-wall shelters the street facing upon the water. A good breakwater would make Veracruz one of the safest harbors along the Gulf, but such an improvement necessitates a large outlay, and is not likely to be undertaken yet a while in the land of "mañana."

The greater portion of our time was spent in the harbor studying the reefs. As we passed over the clear water a perfect treasure-house of nature's wonders could be seen beneath the surface. Corals were growing in rich profusion, and animal life of all kinds was very abundant. Here, over a sandy spot, was crawling a large Triton, a trumpet shell; there, just beneath the surface, were several beautifully colored fishes swimming lazily along; the corals looked very beautiful growing; the Madreporas, with their

CITY OF VERACRUZ

PLATE XV

broad, palmate fronds, and the Meandrinas, with their rounded, pavement-like outlines, stretching far away under the water. With the corals that were brought up by our diver came mollusks, echinoderms, worms, crabs, and a host of marine animals, all of which were transferred to our collecting cans. With what curiosity and expectation we watched the diver beneath the ocean as he patiently pulled and tugged away at a specimen, and how quickly we leaned forward and took the treasure from his hands lest he should damage it!

The reefs in the harbor of Veracruz consist of a number of detached islands from less than half a mile to a mile and a half in length, which extend eastward from the coast line for a distance of nearly six miles. They are known as the Gallega (on which is built the castle of San Juan), Galleguilla, Blanquilla, Anegada de Adentro, Isla Verde, Islote de Pajaros, and Sacrificos. Of these, the Gallega is the largest, measuring in a north-and-south direction considerably over a mile. In view of the peculiar conditions which surround these reefs, it is difficult to understand how it has come to be the general belief among scientists that coral reefs are not found in the western waters of the Gulf of Mexico. Neither Darwin nor Dana mention their existence.

Few recollections of my Mexican rambles are more vivid and agreeable than those of my many walks over the white sea of sand bordering the shore. Far out at sea the white waves were seen breaking over the coral reefs, and in some places dashing high in the air in a sheet of foam as it struck some large barrier. At our feet the waves were rolling in with that soft, ripply murmur so characteristic of a sandy ocean beach. A little way out the sea birds were flying about, and stranded on a reef a mile or more from shore was a large vessel, which had been blown there but a few months ago by a norther. Far, fàr out at sea were seen several vessels, one a large steamer with a column of black smoke pouring from her smoke-stack. The beach was strewn with all manner of débris thrown up by the storms. Lively little crabs were always very abundant, and at every step one would start up and run for his hole in the sand, and if I did not venture to pursue would remain near it and stare at me, his curious stalked eyes moving up and down in a very comical manner.

Marine animals were quite abundant about Veracruz. Among the corals the *Madreporas, Porites, Orbicellas, Diplorias,* and *Siderastræas* were common. The absence of Gor-

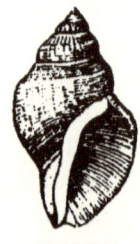

gonias was very noticeable, and only one species was seen (*Plexaura Gorgonia*) *flexuosa*), and this not in great abundance. The large fields of Gorgonias, which so beautify the waters of the reefs of many of the West India islands, were wanting here and with it, of course, the host of brilliantly colored forms associated with them.

PURPURA
HÆMASTOMA.

Among the Echinoderms *Diadema setosum, Echinometra subangularis,* and *Mellita pentapora,* were exceedingly abundant. The mollusks were the most common, and several hundred species were obtained. Such species as *Purpura hæmastoma Floridana, Ricinula nodulosa, Coralliophila abbreviata, Conus mus,- Columbella nitida* were the most numerous in individuals. In the swamp near the city, *Ampullaria* and *Planorbis* was abundant. Land mollusks were very rare. *Helix griseola, Liguus princeps,* and a single *Succinea* were the only forms found. Seven species of crustacea were found, all Decapods, among which was one new form, *Penæus Brasiliensis, var Aztecus.* The vertebrates were scarce, the vultures being about all of this group which we saw, besides a few sea birds.

May 31st we packed our specimens, bade good-bye to our friends in the city, and embarked on the steamship Yumuri for New York, via Progreso and Havana. Our journey homeward was without any notable event, save one, and that a sad one. Among our passengers were a number of musicians who had been travelling with Orin's circus. One of these men was suffering with delirium tremens, and had been placed under surveillance; but one afternoon, when we were at dinner, he eluded his guard and jumped overboard. Although every effort was made to find him it was of no avail, and the steamer was obliged to proceed on her journey without him. The event cast a gloom over the rest of the passengers for several days. Ten days later we arrived in Philadelphia, where we were warmly welcomed, and congratulated upon our safe return from a long but delightful journey through the most inter· esting portion of the Mexican Republic.